PRAISE FOR CHERYL WOLVERTON

"This tender tale...is a suspenseful
and enjoyable read."
—*Romantic Times* on *Shelter from the Storm*

"A captivating delight. *Among the Tulips*
is a heartwarming Cinderella story for
the keeper shelf. (4½ stars)"
—*Romantic Times*

"What an incredible, spiritual journey for readers."
—*Romance Reader on the Run* on *A Wife for Ben*

"Ms. Wolverton's love of writing and joy in God once
again shines through *In Search of a Hero*."
—*Scribesworld*

"*For Love of Zach* delivers a great beginning that
gains momentum all the way to the conclusion."
—*Romantic Times*

"Ms. Wolverton does a lovely job of demonstrating
how two Christians turn to the Lord for help with
their innermost struggles in this warm,
touching and fun book."
—*Romantic Times* on *A Father's Love*

Books by Cheryl Wolverton

Love Inspired

A Matter of Trust #11
A Father's Love #20
This Side of Paradise #38
The Best Christmas Ever #47
A Mother's Love #63
For Love of Zach #76
For Love of Hawk #87
What the Doctor Ordered #99
For Love of Mitch #105
Healing Hearts #118
A Husband To Hold #136

In Search of a Hero #166
†*A Wife for Ben* #193
†*Shelter from the Storm* #198
Once Upon a Chocolate Kiss #229
Among the Tulips #257

Love Inspired Suspense

†*Storm Clouds* #7

*Hill Creek, Texas
†Everyday Heroes

CHERYL WOLVERTON

RITA® Award finalist Cheryl Wolverton has well over a dozen books to her name. Her very popular Hill Creek, Texas, series has finaled in many contests. Having grown up in Oklahoma, lived in Kentucky, Texas, Louisiana and now living once more in Oklahoma, Cheryl, her husband of more than twenty years and their two children, Jeremiah and Christina, always considered themselves Oklahomans, transplanted to grow and flourish in the South. Readers are always welcome to contact her at P.O. Box 106, Faxon, OK 73540, or e-mail at Cheryl@cherylwolverton.com. You can also visit her Web site at www.cherylwolverton.com.

CHERYL WOLVERTON

STORM CLOUDS

Steeple
Hill®

Published by Steeple Hill Books™

STEEPLE HILL BOOKS

Steeple
Hill®

ISBN 0-373-44223-8

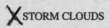

X STORM CLOUDS

Printed in U.S.A.

Brethren, I do not count myself to have apprehended: but one thing I do, forgetting those things which are behind, and reaching forward to those things which are ahead, I press toward the goal for the prize of the upward call of God in Christ Jesus.

—*Philippians* 3:13–14

To my dear Australian friends at Harlequin,
since chatting with you in e-mail, I have
always hoped to set a book in your country.
You guys are the greatest!

Also to my friends online: Aussie, aka Lisa from
ChristianRmWriters, who read my story to correct
me on anything wrong—so if you find mistakes,
as I'm sure you will, they're mine.

And to my mom—it's so much fun to live nearby
again after twenty years and have you getting
on me for missing a day of writing!

And as always to my dear kids, who are now
adults, Christina, twenty-one and Jeremiah,
eighteen and to my husband, Steve.

And finally, Steve's dad, John, for giving us this
wonderful eighty-eight-acre farm to live on—
a place that truly inspires my life and writing.

You guys have been wonderful
through this entire book. Thanks.

Prologue

You're coming here, Angelina. You have no idea what you're walking into. I've waited a long time for this and I'm not going to let you get in the way this time. Oh, no, not this time. I can kill two birds, as the saying goes. Angelina Harding. It's been a long time. And you're coming right to me here in Australia. You'll be within my grasp. Though this is going to put a kink in my plan, you're finally going to be mine. Time to play the mind games—again. And you won't even know it.

Come on, Angie, doll. I'm waiting. Come on and try to find your brother and walk into the maze of my own making. Search for him and play awhile, before you die.

Chapter One

The fuss over her pistol was not the most auspicious start to Angelina Harding's flight. They'd made her check it—fortunately she had a smaller bag she could unzip from her backpack and check.

She'd gotten no sleep on the ride over, but she needed to be here for her brother.

Oh, how she wanted to be back in Pride, Louisiana, the tiny little town with a population of less than one hundred. She'd lived there for three wonderful years, with several of her friends who'd started a security firm. She liked it there in the small town, and she didn't want to venture out into the real world.

But what could she do when she got the

call...a call she hadn't expected? She hadn't talked to her brother in over fifteen years, and he needed her help.

Stepping into the cool air of Australia, she realized she hadn't dressed for spring but late summer.

It was hot as an oven in Baton Rouge.

And it was just finishing winter here.

She shivered and cupped her hand over her eyes to glance toward the sunny sky. Wearily she grabbed a handful of her dark hair, tied it in a knot at her neck and then released it when she realized it had been shading the back of her neck.

Taking a deep breath, she paused to slip her pistol back into her ankle holster, rearrange her backpack and find the paper containing the information she'd jotted down about her brother.

Her internal clock told her it should be nighttime.

Her brother had said catch a plane to Sydney—and to hurry. Like she should drop everything for him. Glancing around, she noted the cars driving on the wrong side of the road.

She'd been so angry with her brother when he'd become a Christian nearly twenty years ago and decided to move to Australia....

She shook her head as she watched the hustle and bustle. Same as in any city but different too. Not seeing her brother, she started down the sidewalk looking for any sign of him. Bitterness nipped at her as she remembered her one visit to Australia when she was sixteen. She'd come here to see her brother.

He had sent her back home, telling her she shouldn't have stolen money from her uncle and should have gotten his permission.

Permission!

She'd hated her brother for not letting her stay, and yet, he was her brother and when he called, she couldn't ignore him as he had her.

Oh, man, she didn't want to be here. Maybe Providence had been trying to keep her from coming. Maybe she should have turned around and left when the airline had hassled her about the gun.

The beep of a horn when she accidentally stepped out in front of a taxi brought her back to the present.

She hated Australia.

Or at least hated what it stood for.

Where was her brother?

Glancing around at the noisy area, she only wanted to be somewhere else.

Her brother's decision to leave her in that forsaken place they'd both called home—at the mercy of her drunken uncle—had stuck with her all these years, haunting her dreams at night when she was all alone in the dark, scary night.

Her brother had left her because he felt called to become a missionary out in the bush of Australia—to start up a church. But in leaving to follow his calling, he'd left her to fend for herself. He didn't mind being alone. She wouldn't have minded being alone either. It would have been better than dealing with her uncle.

She didn't like to remember that time of her life, but coming to Australia forced those memories back into the forefront of her mind.

She hadn't talked to her brother in years because of that incident. She hadn't seen him either.

And now he was in trouble.

Deciding her brother had forgotten to pick her up, she looked for a taxi to hail.

"Angelina Harding?"

She heard her name called and, in surprise, turned.

A man of medium build, dark hair, dark trousers and shirt stood about ten feet away. She was used to cataloguing whomever she met because of her training. A small mole under his right eyebrow barely showed above the sunglasses he wore.

"That would be me," she acknowledged, noting he stood near a large sedan with a driver in it. She couldn't see much else through the tinted windows.

"Your brother sent us."

Her eyebrows shot up and she glanced at the car again. "He must be doing better than I realized," she muttered to the man, feeling that much more angry and put out by her brother. Swinging her backpack over her shoulder, because she refused to pack more than one small case when she traveled, she headed toward the car.

"Let me take your bag," the man murmured and reached out for it.

She shook her head and cradled the bag closer, wrapping her arms around it. "I'm fine."

His hand brushed her side and she stepped away, not liking to be touched and wondering if all were so informal here.

Curious, she glanced at him but he'd turned away.

She sighed.

Her shoulders hurt, her neck ached. All she

wanted to do was crawl into bed, nap and try to adjust to the time change. "I can't believe it," she said as she climbed into the back seat. "He called me and demanded I show up here. Said he had to talk to me. Do you know what I dropped to be here?" She knew the man wasn't listening as he closed the door.

He hesitated again then climbed into the front. Okay, so she was being a grouch and she realized it. But seeing this car really ticked her off. How could her brother afford something like this? It just went to show her that he was so high and mighty now, he expected to have everyone at his beck and call.

She sagged back against the soft cushions of the expensive car.

When someone makes it sound like a matter of life and death, it *usually* means there is something serious the matter, she thought, disgruntled. She'd been in the Secret Service and didn't throw terms like that around idly. In frustration, she closed her eyes and laid her head back on the seat. She had really expected him to be the one to meet her at the airport. And losing it wasn't going to help the situation. *She* had decided to come down here, after all, so whatever happened was just going to happen.

She'd gotten a quick look at the driver as she'd crawled in. He was dressed the same as his companion. She saw in the rearview mirror his blue eyes, however. Very blue. Bluer than the Australian sky.

The buttery leather cushioned her body and invited her to rest. When had Marcus been able to afford such a car? And why had he sent a car for her instead of picking her up himself?

The car pulled smoothly out of the airport and headed out of town. Angelina swayed with the motion of the vehicle. She rested and allowed her aching body to ease as they got under way.

And as they drove, her mind drifted to her brother. All of those years ago he'd lived in a tiny ranch house, no air conditioning, dusty, out in the middle of nowhere. He'd had a group of people who lived with him. Marcus had planned to start up a school for children out in the area. He had even bought a van to pick them up. They were scraping by, but her brother had been so excited. This was his *calling* as he'd labeled it.

Some calling, she thought sourly. Going out into the middle of nowhere to teach kids with an accent.

There were plenty of kids in America with accents if that's what he liked.

She knew she was bitter. But she'd needed her brother, and he hadn't been there. However, he needed her now and she was determined she'd be there for him. Regardless.

When her friend Joshua Staring had started a new security firm in his hometown of Baton Rouge, it had sounded like just what she wanted—what she needed. It was *her* calling, she thought sourly. After all, one could only take so much adrenaline rush, and when the vice-president had almost been shot under her watch, that was it for her. She was glad to be working for Joshua. Mostly.

Angelina frowned and adjusted in her seat when they hit a bump, realizing she'd dozed a bit.

She had many friends in Baton Rouge at the security firm, but most of them were Christians now, and she just didn't fit in with their beliefs. Just like her brother. They thought one way and she another, because she knew the harsh reality of life.

The smell of aftershave reached her nostrils, distracting her from her thoughts. Her brow creased as she forced herself into a more conscious state. Her sour mood faded as she concentrated on the smell. She couldn't remember the name but knew it was quite expensive.

Something niggled at her. Expensive car, expensive cologne. What was her brother into?

Cracking open her eyelid she glanced again at the two men in the front seats; neither had said a word. As she did, she noted something else. She'd been daydreaming longer than she realized for they were now outside of town. And the sun was on the wrong side of the car.

They were headed in the wrong direction.

Angelina might have only been here one other time, but she knew her directions.

Alarm bells went off inside her. "Um, excuse me," she said to draw the attention of the man in the front seat. "How long before we get to where my brother is?"

The man shrugged. "Thirty minutes." Then a window between them slowly rose.

Now fully alert, she sat up. She did her best to keep her expression nonchalant as she glanced out the window because she saw the driver watching her closely. She nodded. "No problem. It's been many years. Just wondered."

Something wasn't right, and she knew if she didn't get out of the car, she wasn't going to see her brother.

Call it instinct. Call it woman's intuition. Call

it experience. She knew that when her insides screamed danger like this, it meant *listen up*.

There was nothing near the car. Mountains in the distance and desert on either side. She knew Australia wasn't like this everywhere and wondered why her brother had chosen such a place to work. He'd told her it had its own beauty.

Right now, it only looked deserted to her. If she tried to escape she just knew that these men had guns and would shoot her.

No one else was in sight for miles.

What was she going to do?

If she were Josh, she'd pray, but then she didn't do that. Her friend back home was always telling her she needed to lean on God. She'd seen too much to believe that.

She needed to think.

And then she saw it.

In the distance, from a road crossing through the rocky terrain, a dust trail arose.

Someone was approaching. She forced herself to stay totally relaxed so not to alert the men in the front seat.

Studying them, she noted the looks they exchanged and knew beyond any doubt that these men weren't from her brother. Had she not been so immersed in her own memories, her instincts would have alerted her much sooner. The dust trail might be her only chance of escape.

If she could time it just right, she could get away and possibly live to find out what was going on.

She leaned back and closed her eyes to slits so the driver would relax his vigil. And she waited.

As they drove onward down the road, the dust trail got closer.

It seemed like hours, but she knew better. A minute, maybe two at most had crept past.

And then they were approaching the place the other vehicle would cross. It wasn't really a road, but more ruts in a dusty trail. She could see the Jeep now plainly.

Taking a quick breath, she wrapped her hand around her backpack, inching her other hand to where she kept her pistol.

When the car was just where it needed to be, she acted. With a quick motion, she pulled out her 9 mm and shot the window to her side. Throwing up her feet, she slammed them into the shattered glass.

She felt the jolt of the car as the driver jerked the wheel in surprise, heard the shouts and the sound of the window between them starting down.

She didn't wait, but pulled her feet under her and shoved herself out the small open space.

Her body hit the hard ground, bouncing painfully over sticks and rocks and whatever else they had out there in the brush as she rolled away from the car. And she lost her gun in the process.

The Jeep swerved, nearly hitting her. The sound of tires squealing, rocks and dust flying, the taste of dirt and smell of fuel all filled the air.

The car she'd bailed out of skidded to a stop, its tires a deeper shriek.

She didn't wait to see what they'd do. With a fast glance around, she noted her pistol wasn't in sight. Growling in frustration, she shoved against the rough dried-out brush as she staggered to her feet, feeling fire blazing down her right arm and right hip where she'd hit the ground. It didn't slow her down, however, as she sprinted across the uneven ground toward the stunned driver of the Jeep.

"Are you all right?" the stranger asked, jumping out of his vehicle and heading toward her.

"Drive!" she shouted and leapt for the car.

Bullet holes appeared in the front panel of the vehicle.

The blond man's eyes widened and he bounded back around to the driver's side and piled in.

Only then did she realize it was some sort of official vehicle.

Shots rang out again.

"If you don't get going we're both going to be dead!"

"Where!" With a sharp twist of the wheel, he jammed it into gear and spun it away from the danger, not waiting for an answer as he turned.

"Away from them!" She started searching for anything to shoot back at the car.

The man didn't hesitate, but popped the car into gear and tore off back the way he'd come.

Angelina flew back into the seat, her head landing with a thud against the headrest. A grunt escaped her. At least he was driving now.

The other car peeled out and she knew that the chase had just begun.

And once again, she wondered just what her brother had gotten himself involved in. If they didn't escape these men, she wasn't going to find out.

Chapter Two

David Lemming pushed the Jeep as fast as he could away from their pursuers, not worried if he broke an axle. He only wanted to put distance between them and the men chasing the crazy woman.

Glancing into the rearview mirror, he saw the car was still following. It hit a bump, bounced up and then back down, smashing against the open range of the reserve. "Care to tell me why they're after you?" he shouted over the loud roar of the engine and wind as they raced madly across the rocky terrain. He swerved to avoid a particularly stout bush and then swerved back to avoid a dip in the landscape.

"I don't know," she shouted in reply. She fell

back into the seat and grabbed at it to keep her balance while her left hand searched his vehicle. David cast a wary glance at her as she rummaged about, bumping him, distracting him... Her eyes suddenly gleamed. She'd found his rifle under the seat. "Hey!" he cried, his utter shock at being shot at suddenly replaced by the fear of this crazy woman getting hold of his gun. "I don't think you should use that."

Sweat broke out on the back of his neck. How had he gotten himself into this situation? He'd been out doing his rounds for the National Park Reserve and then this woman had fallen out of a car. In all of his years and all of his jobs he'd never had something like this happen.

Now he was being chased across the reserve and the woman he'd rescued—or who had hijacked him, he still wasn't sure which—was getting ready to shoot at the people behind them, the people who were trying to kill her...no *them,* he corrected, since he was in the car with this lady. On top of it all, he was having to use every bit of his skill to keep from overturning them as he cut out across the land.

"I know what I'm doing," she warned him as she turned in her seat and braced herself, one knee wedged in the seat as she fought for steadiness and shouldered the rifle.

He suddenly realized the woman wasn't from here. She had a different accent. He tried to place it and groaned when he realized she was one of those loony Americans. Yeah, she probably did know how to use it. They all had guns over there.

They hit a nasty bump and the woman's arm bounced. The rifle went flying.

She let off with a loud shout, very unladylike. "Idiots!"

He winced. "Er, be that as it may, lady, I'd hold on."

She looked at him. "Don't tell me my word choice bothers you? We're about to be killed."

He shrugged. He'd done plenty of drinking and name-calling in his life as a teenager, but now...not now. That wasn't what he'd been wincing over, however. It was the fact that he'd almost lost the woman out the door. Forcing his heart back down out of his throat, he croaked out, "Hold on," and cut sharply to the right.

"We've got to get rid of them!" the woman ordered working to twist back around.

The lady was good at keeping her balance as

fresh bullets whizzed by them. He said a prayer that God would protect them.

That's when an idea came to him. "I think I know a place we can lose them," he called out.

"I'm open to suggestions," she shot back.

He nodded, not understanding what she meant, since he was the one driving. "We're coming up on these canyons." He nodded to where the terrain was rising up on each side of them. "I know a path through..."

"They'll follow," she argued.

He glanced at her and thought that for someone in trouble, she was pretty argumentative. She had turned and was putting her seat belt on.

"Trust me," he said.

She glared at him. "I don't trust anyone."

He wasn't sure how to take that. He concentrated on the curves instead of the woman. The shooting had stopped for the time being since the other car couldn't get a clear shot. "When we get around this next corner I need you to hold on," he called out.

She nodded and braced herself.

He took a deep breath and prayed he didn't kill them both.

A sharp U-turn and he took a path opposite to

the way he'd been going and continued, right to the edge of the road—and then over.

The woman screamed.

He couldn't help but let out a shout as adrenaline rushed through his body.

They crashed down over the side, rattling him from his feet to his teeth. He slammed on the brake and the woman slid forward.

With quick agility, David shoved the gear into Reverse and backed up until he was inside one of the numerous caves in the area. He kept going until they were back beyond anyone's ability to see inside to where they were.

Above them, they heard the car racing past.

He held his breath, waiting, but didn't hear them returning. He could only hope they'd bought it.

Turning toward the woman, he started to say something, pausing when he suddenly realized she was awfully calm considering what he'd just done. His curiosity turned to alarm when he realized the woman was lying back against the seat, still and quiet. "Lady?" He reached over and touched her cheek.

It was wet. And she didn't respond to his touch.

Cold fear shot through him as he realized the passenger was injured.

He opened the glove compartment and found his flashlight. Flipping it on, he saw instantly she'd hit her head. Blood trickled from just below her hairline.

He released his seat belt and turned to grab the first aid kit he kept in the Jeep. It was too easy for things to happen out there so he always kept a kit with him. Fishing through it, he found what he wanted.

Heartened when the woman next to him groaned and moved, he asked, "Can you hear me?" He pulled out some gauze and bandages.

She groaned again.

He reached up to push her long dark hair back behind her ear so he could examine the wound more closely.

She grabbed his hand and nearly broke his fingers.

He jerked back and she pulled him forward.

Immediately he leaned into the fight and pinned her. "Calm down, my little wombat," he whispered.

It must have been his voice or maybe she was finally regaining consciousness completely because she stiffened and then relaxed, releasing him. "Sorry," she muttered and in the dim light, he saw her wince.

"Be still. Let me bandage that head."

It was cool in the cave and he felt the woman shiver. He reached behind her seat and grabbed the jacket he'd worn earlier. "Here, sweetheart, wear this."

"I'm no one's sweetheart," she objected.

He smiled slightly. "Still feisty." Tearing open the gauze, he pulled it out of the package and then placed it over the small laceration. Taking the second one out of the package, he started wiping up the blood from her face. "I don't think this is as bad as it looks."

"You're not the one with the pounding head." Her deep voice echoed, a bit put off at the moment. He would be too, he reminded himself, if he'd just been hurt as she had.

As he wiped her face, high cheekbones revealed themselves on a long angular face. She was quite beautiful. And those deep-brown eyes...

"Done yet?" she grouched at him.

Pulled back to the business at hand, he tossed the bloody gauze and grabbed the roll of first aid tape. Firmly taping the fresh gauze over her wound, he paused to reach out and pull her hair from behind her ear.

Her gaze shot to his as if he'd done something of which she didn't approve.

He admitted it was a very intimate gesture, but he'd had to touch the soft hair once again.

Sitting back, he studied the woman carefully, working to break the intimacy of his gesture. "I'm David Lemming. And you are?"

"Hurting from head to toe," she answered. "Got any painkillers in that box?"

He lifted a brow at the way she'd avoided answering then reached in and pulled out some medication, which he handed to her. She didn't blink, but slipped it into her mouth and swallowed without water.

He swallowed, his own throat dry. He felt a bit like choking as he watched her.

She glanced ahead and then finally cut a quick glance at him. "Angelina Harding."

He nodded. Turning around to face the front as she did, he stared toward the bright dusty exit to their inner sanctum. "You were unconscious when they passed, but they have long since gone on down the road."

"They'll be back," she warned.

He thought about that. Curious, he asked, "Why are they after you?"

She sighed and leaned back against the head-rest. "I honestly don't know, but I'm afraid it might have something to do with my brother."

Though that made no sense to him, he didn't ask for more information. "I need to call the authorities." He snagged the radio in the car to call in—and saw the bullet holes. Consternation forced a temporary scowl to his face. "Well, that's out."

"Don't you have a cell phone?" she asked. "I need to check on my brother."

Incredulous he turned to look at her. He shook his head. He wasn't even going to answer that one. "Where is your brother?"

"Wallabee."

Surprised, he said, "Here in Australia? But you sound American."

She nodded and raised a hand to her sore head obviously regretting the action. "He lives here. A missionary."

David felt shock down to his toes. She'd said her name was Angelina Harding. *Harding*. He knew that name well, at least the last name, but until she'd said what her brother did, he hadn't made the connection. Still, he couldn't believe this beauty might be connected to the sweet quiet and yet homely man he knew. "Not Marcus Harding?"

She glanced at him and there was acknowledgement in her eyes. "You know my brother?"

Slowly, he nodded. "He led me to the Lord just about ten years ago."

Her face twisted up as if she'd just tasted something sour.

"Great." She looked him up and down. "So you're one of those Christians too." She leaned back into the chair and muttered "Just great."

Surprised, he sat back. Marcus didn't mention his sister much. Only that she'd moved, not keeping in touch with him and that he only heard about her occasionally. Things of that sort. "You're his sister."

"We've already established that."

"What were you doing in that car?"

She sighed again, definitely in a worse mood than only a moment before—and all because he'd said he was a Christian.

"Okay. Here's the quick version. My brother called me yesterday and insisted he needed me over here as soon as possible. It was some national emergency or something. We don't talk much," she added acidly. "Anyway, I rushed over here. Instead of him meeting me at the airport, these two goons show up and say my brother has sent them. Obviously, my brother hasn't taken a hit out on me so he didn't send them. Which means something must have happened to my brother. I need to get in touch with him as soon as possible."

He watched the fluctuating emotions in her eyes and felt for her. Though she sounded angry and sarcastic, there was an underlying edge of worry in her voice and hurt in her eyes.

Compassion flooded him. "I can get you there. First thing first, however, sweetheart. I think we should get your head examined."

She shot him a look.

He lifted his hands. "What?"

"That's not a good way to say that. And I don't need this small bump examined anyway. I need to see my brother."

He frowned. "We'll need to call the authorities."

He could tell she wasn't thrilled with that idea. "Fine. But we'd better get out of here before those men find us."

He nodded. Reaching for the key, he turned it—and nothing happened.

"What's the matter?" Angelina asked immediately.

David shrugged. He turned it again and there was only a low grinding sound. Battery light showed fine, temperature was okay… "We're out of petrol," he said and stared at the gauge.

"You're kidding!" She scoffed and then leaned forward to peer at the gauges. Impatiently she tapped the glass over the gauge. It definitely registered empty.

"I just filled up this morning." He shook his head. "That's impossible." He thought about tapping it himself but resisted the urge.

"Yeah," the woman muttered and then groaned when her movement caused fresh pain in her right arm.

He turned the key off and got out of the Jeep. Going around to the side of the vehicle, he reached to open the gas tank and saw the problem.

"What is it?" Angelina asked lowering her hand from her eyes as the pain eased.

She knew already, he thought. If she was used

to this, she surely knew. She was simply mollifying him. "Petrol tank was shot up. Our petrol is all on the ground—what was left, that is."

She sighed. "Figured as much. Well, we can't stay here."

He disagreed, but then thought, if those guys had any brains they would come back looking. He nodded. "Very well. I know the cavern system here. It's a bit cool, but we can follow this for two kilometers and come up away from here which might give us a safer chance to hitch a ride back on the main road."

She shifted and pulled herself out of the Jeep.

David went around and helped her out. Catching her arms, he steadied her as she lowered her feet to the rocky ground. With concern, he asked, "The question is—can you make it, sweetheart?"

She glowered at him. "I can make it, but if you call me sweetheart one more time, you just might not."

He found himself grinning. "A feisty sheila is better than an unconscious one. Follow me, stay conscious and we'll be okay."

She grunted something under her breath, and

his smile widened. Despite the fact that this normal day had turned crazily upside down, he thought he might just enjoy the next hour or two with this woman.

Chapter Three

"Thank you." Angelina nodded to the driver who had given them a ride to her brother's mission. Evidently, many in the area knew her brother.

And as she stepped out of the vehicle, she could see why. This was the first *town* they'd come to since exiting the caves several miles back.

It stretched on for what seemed like forever. It sure hadn't been like this years ago. A simple broken-down house had been all that'd existed. The house was still there, repaired and bigger. But along with that were two huge buildings nearby and a yard, a green landscaped yard that covered the entire area. Cemented walkways led off toward some other buildings and then past those were two large structures that reminded her of college dorms. Though not as nice, they were still impressive. She could see horses running in the distance and what looked like a small golf-cart-type vehicle, not in the best of shape, going down a dirt path between two of the far-off structures.

"Those are men's and women's dorms off in the distance. The three buildings over there are teaching rooms and the barns are over there. This is the house Marcus lives in."

David Lemming was still with her. Her mouth twisted. "I knew that."

He'd asked her why she was here and probed a bit, but when he'd figured out she wasn't in the mood to talk, he'd left her alone. Obviously, he wasn't going to leave her, though. Turning, she asked curiously, "Why are you still here?"

He shrugged. "Marcus is a good friend. It wouldn't be right for me to leave his little sister to fend for herself."

She gaped. Surely, he was kidding. Leave her alone to fend for herself? How sexist. She shook her head. Without a word, she turned on her heel and headed toward the house surrounded by a wooden fence with no real gate. The old-fashioned poles set in an upside down U denoted the entrance to the area.

It was pretty empty looking. The grass in the front yard and a few small flowerbeds added a touch of homey atmosphere, but there was also a watering trough set next to the house and a makeshift separate structure that provided shade for a parked vehicle. She wondered why, if David had fixed up the rest of the campus, he hadn't built himself a new house as well.

The sound of horses in the stables reached her ears. In the distance, she could see students ambling from one of the buildings toward the dorms. Under trees, people young and old rested, chatting, some with books opened or in close discussion.

This was a mission?

"Can I help you?"

Angelina turned her head back toward the house to see a man close to her own age walking forward.

"I'm Angelina Harding. Who's in charge?"

"I'll get Steve." His gaze traveled over her curiously before he turned and strode back to the building. Almost immediately, an older man appeared. Dressed in scruffy pants and a button-down top, boots and a hat, he came forward. He was as dark as midnight, yet had the kindest eyes.

"David!" The man tipped his hat. "I'm Steve Hawkins," he said to Angelina. "You'd be Marcus's sister, wouldn't you?"

She shook his hand, shaken by how nice the man seemed. Forcing her professionalism to the forefront, she nodded. "I received a call from him yesterday. What's going on? Where's Marcus?"

The older man frowned. His gaze darted to David and then back. "I'm afraid I have some bad news, miss." He took his hat off and held it respectfully before him. "Your brother has gone missing."

Angelina blinked. "Excuse me?"

The man glanced at David again.

Irritated she started to correct him but David spoke up. "Has someone called the authorities?"

The man nodded. He motioned with his hat. "Let's get in outta this sun. You'll burn fast down here if you aren't used to it."

He turned and headed to the house.

Numbly, Angelina followed.

After years of being angry with her brother, full

of bitterness, refusing to see him, then she got news like this? She was furious with him, and yet...

"Are you all right?"

She glanced at David and realized he was carefully watching her reaction. She forced her neutral expression back over her features. "Fine. Where are the authorities?"

She stepped into the warm house and realized just how chilled she'd become. Her body immediately reacted to the warmth.

"Ted, get some tea please," Steve called to the man who'd originally greeted them and now stood across the room, rustling through some papers on a table. He looked up, glanced at Angelina again, then nodded and disappeared down a hallway.

Another man stood up, a set of ledgers in his hands. Tall, distinguished, he wore a dark suit and boots.

"This is Frank Henson. Frank, this is Marcus's sister."

Frank nodded. "Sorry about the bad news, Ms. Harding."

"He's one of our financiers. He's been in on your brother's venture since nearly the beginning," Steve explained to Angelina. Turning to Frank, he said, "Can we finish this up later, Frank?"

The gentleman nodded. "Of course. I understand." He studied David curiously and nodded. "David." Then his gaze went back to Angelina. He was probably wondering why she looked as if she'd been dragged through a drain pipe backwards, she thought. He nodded again. "I'll be back later."

He left, going through the back hall that Angelina thought might lead toward the kitchen. Though she'd been here before, she didn't remember everything, some things had faded with time.

Steve led them into the spacious living room and motioned to the sofa.

Angelina didn't realize David had followed until he seated himself by her. Why was he acting so protectively, she wondered.

"Is your head okay, miss, or do I need to get you medical attention?"

"I'm fine—"

"She needs medical attention," David said at the same time.

She scowled at him.

Ted brought in the tea and Steve said something in another language to Ted who replied, then nodded and left. There certainly hadn't been this many people either, back then, Angelina thought, Frank, Ted, Steve…all living here with her brother?

"Ted also helps manage the mission." Steve nodded to the nice-looking man who had slipped out the front door. She saw him glance back one last time and then disappear from sight.

Steve handed a cup of tea to Angelina. "What did the authorities say?" she demanded as soon as Ted was gone.

She didn't want to play tea party. She wanted to find out about her brother.

David accepted the tea and handed it to Angelina. She scowled, but took it, favoring her right arm as she did.

"I was gone last night," Steve began and Angelina wondered if he was purposely trying to ignore her direct question.

Steve passed tea to David and then took his own. He added cream and sugar and stirred. Expressive eyes filled with anger when he finally looked back to her. "I had to run one of the students into town. She'd been feeling bad and the nurse was gone. It was our night out anyway so most of the students were away. Your brother told me to stop and pick up some groceries on the way back for the house, and so I was later than normal getting back—"

"And?" Angelina interrupted. She reached up for her head, realizing she was being rude but really only wanting an answer.

"Forgive me, miss. But I thought you'd want to know why your brother was alone. When I got back, well, the house was empty. Furniture was overturned and some of the lamps broken. We just now only an hour past got the house put to rights."

Despite being separated from her brother for years, Angelina felt the blood drain from her face. Suddenly she was once again that little girl whose uncle used to drag her brother out of the room to *talk* with him. "Someone took him."

David took her tea and set it aside, which snapped her back to the present. She shook herself.

"It looks that way, miss. I called the authorities immediately. They came out and looked around and I told them all that I knew, but…we're praying."

Her scowl returned. "Praying?" She stood. "My brother is missing and you're wasting time praying?"

Steve reacted in shock. "Well we might not know where he is, miss, but God does."

"Please!" She'd had all she could of this bunk. "What did the police say?"

Steve looked a bit nonplussed by her reaction.

"Angelina." David's voice drew her attention. "You might want to let Steve finish his story."

He was another one of those Christians, but the gentleness in his eyes convinced her to hold her tongue. She was out of line.

Turning back to Steve, she took a deep breath and let it out. "I apologize, Steve. Can you tell me anything else?"

He nodded. "Your brother had contacts with all sorts of underworld types because of the life many of our students come from. You know, he'd hang out and meet them as he was helping others. They might not like his ways, but they respected him. He went into the cities and into the bush alike and was always hearing things. He's rather a hero around here. He helped cut crime nearly in half. He'd been out making his rounds when he heard something disturbing. He didn't go into any details with me, but I do know he mentioned you several times and decided he just might ring you up."

"Did he say anything else?"

Steve shook his head. "The authorities asked me the same thing. No, miss. We're hoping Jake might be able to tell us something if he regains consciousness."

"Jake?" David asked.

Surprised, Angelina turned her attention to David.

Steve nodded to David. "When I got back from town, we found this place tore up, and poor Jake was lying in the kitchen unconscious. We think the person or people came in through the back because of the woods and conked poor Jake over the head."

"Who's Jake?" Angelina asked, then turned to David. "And just how do you know *everyone* here?"

David answered this time. "He's the cook. When Marcus led me to the Lord, Jake took me under his wing. He's a special friend. And I used to own all of this land."

"Still do."

David acknowledged the other man's comment.

Angelina didn't ask him to elaborate. Her mind still whirled with the fact that all of these people knew each other and they were all Christians like her brother. She didn't like that.

Putting it aside, she turned back to Steve. "Did my brother ever keep notes? Anything?"

Steve sighed. "The authorities already asked me that and went through his study."

Her brother wouldn't have kept it there. At least not when they were kids. They'd hidden everything from their uncle. "Can I see his bedroom?"

"You need medical attention," David said gently.

She sighed. He was right.

"Ted sent for the nurse," Steve told David.

She bristled. "Then I can search his room while we're waiting for the nurse?"

Her brother, gone. It was starting to sink in that her brother really was missing, and that whatever he'd called her about tied into his disappearance.

Unfortunately, searching his room was going to have to wait as the nurse walked in right then.

Frustration built. "I need to call the police too," she blurted out.

David touched her hand.

She jerked.

"Look sweet—gelina," he corrected. His look calmed her as she stared into his eyes. And the way he'd changed the "sweetheart" almost drew a grin—almost.

Still, that gentle touch anchored her. What had happened to her world in the last twenty-four hours?

"I'll call the authorities and report what has happened. I need to let my boss know why I'm gone as well. You allow the nurse to tend you and then, when someone arrives to take our report, you can question them about your brother. Before that, however, you can search your brother's room. Maybe you'll find something that will help them. All right?"

She didn't want to admit this man's plan made sense. She tilted her head slightly. "How long have I known you now?"

He smiled, dimples appearing. "Too long, I'm afraid."

She chuckled. The man had a sense of humor. "I suppose I should apologize for your Jeep."

"That *is* going to be hard to explain to my boss."

"I'll be glad to elaborate for him."

"Americans," he said softly and chuckled.

She lifted an eyebrow in response, which reminded her of the injury.

"You go this way, miss, and Myra will examine you."

She glanced at the woman who stood quietly off to the side. Large, wide features, but pretty, she had her hair pulled back, wore a pair of faded jeans and a top tucked in with a brown belt. She carried a knapsack in one hand.

Definitely not what she expected a nurse to look like.

Maybe if she got her alone, she could find out a bit more of what was going on, or what had been going on. She glanced at David. "Sounds like a plan."

David nodded. "Go with her then."

She stood and David watched her go. When she was gone, he turned to Steve.

"How are you feeling?" Steve asked.

David picked up his tea and drank some. The heat felt good going down his throat. "Like I've been run over by my Jeep," he answered when he was done with the hot liquid.

"How did you end up with Marcus's sister?"

"That's a story," David said. He stood and

paced to the window. His back and shoulders ached from going over that cliff. He still couldn't believe he'd done that and laid that at God's feet. It had just come to him in a small voice to do it— and they had survived. Of course, they were both sore—but alive and sore were better than the alternative. "I was out making my rounds when this woman came flying out a window of a passing vehicle. I honestly thought the little sheila had tried to kill herself until she jumped up and ran toward me. Bullets exploded about us so I started driving." He turned and faced Steve. "How did an American—and not just any American, but Marcus' sister—end up out there in the middle of nowhere?"

"God's will," Steve said simply.

"It must have been. I was the only vehicle for kilometers. They shot up the boot and filled the Jeep with holes. I had no petrol left." He ran a hand through his short sandy hair and sighed. "And I have no idea if the people who were chasing her are still after us. I kept looking over my shoulder the entire time. All I could think was we had to get out of there and get here before something happened to Angelina."

Why he'd felt that way, he wasn't sure. But it

had been his little wombat he'd worried about instead of himself. She was spirited. And when he'd touched her face in the cave… His blunt fingers had looked so large against her small delicate features. He'd wanted to fix all of her problems, even though he hadn't known who she was. That was his purpose for being where he'd been.

Steve nodded. "Marcus would appreciate that. I know he's never forgiven himself for not bringing Angelina with him."

David nodded. Marcus rarely talked of his sister except to say they came from a bad background, and more was going on with Angelina than he'd understood at the time. David wasn't sure what that meant, only that years later Marcus had regretted leaving Angelina in the States. He wondered how Marcus could have left such an innocent to fend for herself, though she was spunky and could handle a gun. "I need to call the authorities."

Steve nodded and David went to the phone and rang up the nearest help. When he was off the phone, he turned back to Steve, who perused him and said, "You look a bit injured yourself."

David glanced down. "I'm dirty, but the blood is from Angelina. What a sheila," he said and shook his head. "I'm battered and bruised but I don't think I have any other injuries."

Steve nodded. "Still," he said sipping his tea, "you should get checked out."

David sank down to the couch. "After Angelina's done, then. Tell me, why would they grab Marcus and not you, since you both run this mission?"

Steve shook his head and his features became inscrutable. "I don't know. You know I do a lot of the tending and counseling, but Marcus is the more evangelistic of the two of us. Shari asked me the same thing," he said referring to his wife who lived in their house about a kilometer away. "She was terrified for me to come to work today. But let me ask you something. Since you're a millionaire, why didn't they grab you?"

David shrugged. "It obviously doesn't have anything to do with money. I don't think they knew who I was." He was glad Angelina didn't pick up on Steve's mention of him owning the land or ask him why he was working at such a job if he was so rich. It was a God thing. He needed this time to search and the job gave him joy—a break from his former life while he considered his future.

"Well, if Angelina is here and Marcus is missing and I've somehow been brought into this, I guess I'd better call my work and tell them I won't be in for a while."

Steve smiled softly. "Think maybe all this time off searching is finally leading you to your destiny?"

David scoffed, "I'm not called to the ministry and no, Marcus's sister is definitely not my destiny. I do think, however, that maybe, since Marcus is like a brother to me, I should watch out for his sister until we can find him." He knew he was contradicting what he'd said, but he wouldn't admit to Steve that he felt protective of this strange woman.

Steve simply smiled and David found himself scowling much as Angelina had done only a short time before. No, his destination was still his own. He knew what God wanted him to do. Working alone in the reserve by himself was fine. Why Steve insisted that there was more he didn't know. But he did know, as much as Marcus meant to him, he couldn't let Angelina run around his country unattended—and he had a feeling if someone didn't keep an eye on her that was exactly what would happen.

So God had sent her his way and he was going to make sure she was safe until they could find Marcus.

He only wondered if Angelina would comply. He doubted she was complying with whatever the nurse was doing right now, either.

Chapter Four

Idiots!

You don't know who they are, do you? But now you know someone is after you as well.

It won't be those same men, though. No, Angie, doll. One of them is being disposed of right now because you made me lose my temper.

You won't best me again. This isn't just about my plan now, but it's about you as well.

You now know your brother is missing. Yes, I saw you pull up to the compound. And you didn't even recognize me. I thought I was going to have to kill you immediately. Amazing. You're slipping up. Just how much are you still with the game? Will you find the clues left behind? Clues that will

*lead you far from your brother? Come on, Angie,
look hard. Find the little crumbs of bread I've laid
out for you to follow... Right into my trap.*

Chapter Five

～

She'd endured the nurse's ministrations. She'd needed two small stitches in her hairline—not the first time she'd had that happen. She'd actually had to sew herself up a couple of times when she'd been out in the field. And once her partner had needed stitches.

She'd had little time for the nurse—especially as she'd prattled on and on about God.

Her boss and her friends mentioned religion but never pushed. But that was all they talked about here. She didn't remember it being like this ten years before—but then she'd been running and scared, so anything would have been better than where she'd come from. And back then, she might have actually been interested—

before her brother had turned her away, before she'd gone back and faced her uncle.

She forced her mind away from the past. She'd gotten over that. She'd gone through therapy and knew it wasn't her fault. She could handle herself fine.

"Find anything?"

She heard the voice behind her and jumped. How had he sneaked up on her? Turning, she lifted an eyebrow. "What are you doing here?"

David smiled that gentle smile that unnerved her. "I brought you here remember?"

She scowled. "You know what I meant."

His smile turned crooked. "I called my boss. He's quite upset about the Jeep."

He was trying to make her feel guilty, she realized, and it was working. Turning back to her brother's room, she went back to searching his dresser.

"But don't worry, I explained everything," David continued. He hadn't moved from by the doorway. "My boss thinks I'm suffering hallucinations so he's given me some time off."

She whirled back around.

He chuckled. "Not really. I did take some vacation, however."

Her eyes widened. "Why?"

"You need help."

"I do not need assistance," she informed him. "I used to work in security." She didn't want to tell him Secret Service. "I can handle myself."

She returned to searching and heard his soft tread as his feet crossed the tiled floor and hit the carpet.

"Are all Americans this stubborn?"

His voice was deep and melodic. He could be an announcer for a radio. She looked up in the mirror at his reflection. "That's so cliché."

He shrugged. "I've never been to America."

"And all Australians live in dusty wastelands and have kangaroos as pets, I assume?" she replied.

He chuckled. "As a matter of fact, we do have a few kangaroos on the property here, but sorry, back at my flat in Fleting, I have no kangaroos."

"Fleting?"

"Not too far from Wallabee actually," he informed her.

Realizing she had been distracted, she focused back on the dresser.

"Where have you searched?" he asked and backed off.

"All of the usual places. I haven't found anything." She jerked open the top drawer where she remembered her brother's cuff links being stored and blinked.

"What have we here?" David asked, curiously and moved forward.

"Looks like an address book. But why wouldn't the police have found this?" She pulled it out and opened it. It wasn't an address book, but had notes jotted in it. People's names, descriptions of places and such.

"Perhaps because they wouldn't expect something to be stored in there—other than men's tie tacks?"

"Sloppy police work," Angelina muttered.

She went over to a bench that ran under the window and sat down. David followed. Slowly she flipped through page after page. "There's a lot in here I don't understand."

David reached for the book. She allowed him to take it; the professional part of her understood that as a local, he might see something she didn't.

And he did. "Cowboy lingo."

She blinked. "What do you mean by that?"

"That's what you call it isn't it? Ranchers?"

"I know what the word means." She shook her head. "What do you see?"

"This is how we measure off kilometers. And this means Fleting actually and here is an abbreviation for a street in Wallabee. Fleting is a bigger town. I think this might be a nightclub."

"My brother wouldn't go to nightclubs," she argued.

David stopped flipping the pages and looked up at Angelina. "You really don't know much about your brother do you?"

Coolly she replied, "We don't get along."

He started to comment, shook his head and then said, "Let me explain how I met your brother."

"I don't see—"

"It has to do with the nightclub."

She hesitated. Time was ticking away. Her brother was missing, and this man wanted to share stories with her. But she'd learned in her business it was better to be thorough than to go off half-cocked. If she wanted to find her brother, she was going to have to step back and act professionally instead of like a family member.

"Go ahead," she said and forced herself to relax and analyze what he was going to say.

"I used to own a big part of this spread twenty years ago. I was a sheep rancher."

She nodded. Interesting, she thought.

"I had everything any man could want. I'd inherited the business from my dad and mum. They died younger than they should have in a flash flood." Darkness crossed his features and then cleared. "However, we were a very loving family. I was an only child. I had cousins I grew up with who are still around today. Several worked for me and some still work here. I was known as a very hardworking man if I can say that without pride." He flushed a bit. "I also would party quite hard on the weekends.

"But still, despite having everything, I really didn't have anything. I'd wake up on Monday morning hungover, go back to work and repeat the process. Then a young American showed up. He bought this old farmhouse you're in now. I was his nearest neighbor and thought it odd that someone would travel so far to buy this rotting house."

"The nightclub?"

"You certainly are impatient," he said, before growing serious. "Your brother told me that was all he could afford. I felt sorry for the bloke, and, well, I decided to check on him occasionally. I even invited him out to the clubs."

"He wouldn't go," Angelina said.

"Not at first. He wanted to tell me about God. I laughed and told him not too many around these parts went to church because we didn't have time. So he made a deal with me. He agreed to go with me to the nightclub if I'd go with him to the church he was starting up."

"He wouldn't do that," Angelina protested. "He was too straight an arrow."

"Oh, he was a straight arrow all right," David agreed, amused. "He went with me to the nightclubs every night, but it was to pass out literature and to witness to those there. He wouldn't drink. He was a downright bore. But then, I hadn't set up the rules, as he'd informed me. Imagine that? I'm an excellent businessman and yet I didn't set up rules for our outing."

"Well, who would have thought he'd do something like that," Angelina blurted out, flabbergasted. She couldn't imagine her sweet older brother going out to witness in clubs.

"My thoughts exactly. And he was so determined to get these people saved. I didn't understand his angle, to be honest. And that caught my curiosity. So I went with him to church. He held it in the broken-down old barn, the one we rebuilt over there," he waved in the general direction of the outside area where she'd seen two big barns. She didn't remember a barn there, she realized. Of course, she'd been here such a short time.

"He kept talking about this Jesus as if he were a real person interested in your life. It wasn't about church at all, but about doing stuff daily. And then he explained how he was a substitute for my sin…"

Moisture gathered in his eyes and he blinked. "Ya see, sweetheart, that's what my mum and dad did. They saved my life, sacrificing their own. I was really injured in the flood and trapped and wouldn't have made it if my dad hadn't rescued me. My mum caught pneumonia caring for me. I understood sacrifice and substitution. And that grabbed hold of me. I thought keeping the ranch going was a way to repay my parents, but it left me empty inside. It wasn't immediate, but eventually, Marcus led me to a personal relationship with Jesus. And it was all because he agreed to go to the nightclubs with me."

"That sounds nice, but why aren't you ranching now if you were such a rancher before?"

"I leased the land to Marcus for his buildings. I still own it, but he is using it. And I have taken time off, the last year, to find what God intends for me. I used to help run the property and do management. That's how I know Frank. When I went into the venture with your brother, we needed someone who could oversee much of the legalities. Frank was right there, so, he helped set up the deal between your brother and me and it went fine until lately. Now I'm looking for more."

"So, about the nightclubs."

"Yes." David nodded. "Back to the nightclubs. Your brother started going into the bad parts of the nearby towns and reaching the people that most citizens had given up for lost. That's how his ministry has grown so big. As I said, I watched for a long time before I finally gave myself to God and started serving Him, but I'd see him many weekends down ministering on the streets. And I do know that he had a lot of contacts in the area."

He hefted the book in his hand and drew her attention back to it. "I am thinking this is what you've found here."

She took the book and flipped it over in her

hand. The leather was worn and it didn't look like much. Angelina would guess Marcus carried this quite a bit, probably in his back pocket judging by the way it curved. She held on to it, willing the warmth of her brother's presence into it, but it did no good.

"Miss? The authorities are here."

Steve stood in the doorway.

Curling her fingers around the book, she made a quick decision. Standing, she slipped the book into her own back pocket.

David lifted one blond eyebrow in inquiry but didn't comment. "Are you up to this?"

She nodded. "It's the only way I'm going to find my brother."

She was glad he hadn't asked her about the book.

Leaving the room, she shook off the emotions that had swirled within. Time for professionalism. She had to separate herself from the victim and find out just what was going on.

In the main room she found a very nice-looking woman in pants and a dress jacket sitting on the sofa. She had a small book in which she was writing some notes. She positively exuded authority.

There was a younger man nearby who stood when he saw Angelina.

She ignored him and went to the person clearly in charge. "I'm Angelina Harding," she informed the woman.

The woman stood. About five foot six, the woman catalogued Angeline's features with her blue eyes. "I'm Inspector Washburn. Tina," she added and shook hands. "This is Richards. Steve filled me in some while we waited." She glanced at David with an appraising eye and Angelina noted a brief hint of interest.

"David Lemming." His voice next to her ran down her spine, and she wondered if he'd noted the quick flare of interest as well.

He shook Inspector Washburn's hand. The woman immediately focused on him and was once again purely professional. "You're the one who called in the report?" she asked.

"I am."

Angelina noticed the other inspector had come forward and was writing information on a small pad of paper as well. "Tell me, Ms. Harding. Do you think these men abducting you have something to do with your brother's disappearance?"

She nodded. "I do. It was too coincidental that

someone tried to kidnap me from the airport at the same time my brother had gone missing."

David turned slightly to study her. She knew she hadn't told him much of anything and he burned with curiosity now. She had to applaud him for not interrupting. She wouldn't have put up with such actions if someone had tried to keep her in the dark as she had him. However, she was only now starting to believe she could trust this man. She hadn't been entirely sure he wasn't in on the conspiracy. It seemed too coincidental that he'd been just where she needed him at the right moment.

"And you managed to escape?"

She nodded. "Mr. Lemming helped by being in the right place at the right time."

She noticed Tina's look of interest at that as well. "Good for you, Mr. Lemming."

"I try," David said blandly.

Angelina glanced at him. He wasn't happy with the undertone of suspicion in the inspector's voice. Well, nevertheless, it *was* very coincidental, and the inspector was right to wonder about it. Angelina drew the inspector's attention back to her. "My brother called me. He needed to talk to me—in person. He wouldn't tell me what he wanted. I work in…worked in the Secret Service back in the U.S. and it had something to do with that."

The woman frowned, flipped a page on her notebook and jotted down some notes. Richards was still writing away. "Any idea what?" he asked.

Angelina shook her head. She turned from the woman and paced to the window. "No idea. Our governments don't have that much interaction."

"No, though your president is coming to visit next week," the man added.

Angelina turned sharply.

"You don't keep up on what is going on in your own country?" Inspector Washburn asked in reaction to Angelina's surprise.

"Of course I do, but…" she trailed off. Out here in the bush? What could that have to do with her brother?

"Of course," Tina continued, "I doubt that has anything to do with your brother's disappearance. I am thinking it has to do with the fact that he just appointed a new vice president after your old one was caught in scandal."

Angelina didn't want to think about that. America was still reeling from the fact that their vice president had been caught in arms deals with the enemy. The president had either had to get rid of the vice president or go down with him.

Washburn made a few more notes and closed her notebook. "From what your brother's partner says, you two haven't spoken in years…?"

Angelina nodded, though her mind wouldn't leave the tidbit about the president. Of course, perhaps that was what had triggered the thought of calling her in her brother in the first place. "More than likely something is going on here and my brother, knowing about the visit, thought of me and decided I could help him."

Tina didn't look convinced. "He called you in America to get your help over here?"

More firmly, Angelina nodded. "It makes sense. He knew I'd worked for the current president and you probably have had his visit in the news a lot. He used to watch the news all the time. Seeing it over and over most likely made him think about me—my job. Whatever problem he was having here made him decide he could use my expertise and he called me."

David nodded. "That does make sense."

Steve shook his head. "I just don't know what he was going through. He'd been moody lately, preoccupied. But I didn't think anything about it until he went missing."

Tina nodded. "Very well. You think on the last weeks, Mr. Hawkins," she said to Steve. "If you come up with anything, let us know. And Ms. Harding, if you can give us a description of your assailants and the car, we'll start looking for them, though we are a big area out here and they're probably gone."

Angelina nodded and quickly gave them a description.

"And if you think of anything else, call us." She turned to her partner. "Come on, Richards."

Richards nodded.

Steve escorted them out.

She let out a weary breath. She was bone-tired from the time change and felt as if she'd been trounced by a kangaroo. "Are you going to be all right?"

He was still here.

She turned.

Kind eyes met hers. She didn't feel like arguing. For the first time in a long time she felt like crying—though she never would.

The man in front of her must have sensed something because, shocking her down to her toes, he suddenly reached out and pulled her into his large embrace.

She stiffened, hating his touch—at first. But he didn't let go. "I'm sorry I wasn't more sympathetic earlier, but you have to admit, I felt as if I'd been kidnapped myself."

His arms hugged her like a big bear but strangely enough, he felt safe.

She didn't like that at all. She had never, ever allowed a man this close, not even her boss and friend back home. She pushed against his chest, but he didn't release her. "Shush a moment," he said softly. "I'm trying to apologize."

He felt so good. Man, did he feel good.

Hunger opened up inside her, craving the emotional warmth he offered.

When had she ever allowed anyone, since her brother, to reach past her barriers and touch her like this?

"I accept," she said desperately, only wanting away. She pushed and this time he released her, but when she looked up ready to blast him for holding her, she saw only a puzzled expression on his face.

The words stuck in her dry throat. She shook her head. "I need a short nap and then I'm going to study this book."

She turned and nearly fled toward her brother's room wondering what in the world was happening to her. At least she had finally put some distance between them. Or so she'd thought.

Chapter Six

"This is Wallabee."

David Lemming was refreshed, feeling much better after a shower and in a set of Marcus's clothes. However, he was still puzzled by Angelina's reaction earlier. She kept trying to put distance between them, all the way into town, and perversely enough, he'd taken every chance to get closer or to brush his hand over hers. She puzzled him, and if touching her was the only way to find out more about her, he was more than willing to do that.

"There isn't much here," Angelina protested, looking at the town of about twelve hundred souls.

"We're out in the bush, sweetheart."

She scowled at him. "I don't like that name."

He grinned. The prickly Angelina was back. He wasn't sure which Angelina he liked better. When he'd hugged her earlier back at the mission, something had happened, something very unexpected. Instead of a feisty little wombat, he'd realized he was holding a very attractive, vulnerable woman—one who wasn't used to being touched or comforted.

He'd been totally unprepared for her reaction. She'd stiffened and acted like a 'roo caught in headlights.

She'd been hurt sometime in her life, that was obvious.

He'd wanted to go out and punch something. Who hurt this woman, and why had she been so undone by his touch?

"Where did my brother find all of the people who attend church?" she asked looking around.

He got out of the vehicle and slammed the door. Angelina followed suit. She came around the front of the Rover and propped her hands on her slender hips, looking up at the general mercantile. "We have a lot of ranchers. The town is small, but there are several outlying areas. Plus, as I said, Fleting isn't too far away in the opposite direction."

She nodded. Pulling the tiny book out of her back pocket, she flipped it open.

David moved next to her, where he was close enough to smell the fresh scent of soap from her recent shower. "Curiosity, sweetheart, but why didn't you tell the authorities about the book?"

Angelina paused in flipping the pages to lift her determined gaze to his. She wanted to step back, but he saw her refusal to give ground, afraid it would make her look weak. "Someone wanted me—not the authorities—to find this."

"Someone left it for you?" He scratched his head in confusion. "But who knew you were coming? And why didn't the authorities find it?"

"Unless you have one of the worst police forces around, this wasn't here when they went through the rooms."

A car drove past. David glanced at it. Hooking Angelina by the elbow, he urged her onto the sidewalk. He nodded to someone who hurried by with a child in tow. When they were out of earshot, he turned back to Angelina. "Explain please?"

She glanced coolly around. "Whoever took my brother left this, or had someone leave it, especially for me. They knew I'd search through his things. I met your detectives. They seemed sharp and on target. So it only makes sense that someone wanted me to find this."

"You can't be sure," David argued. The hairs on the back of his neck stood on end at her words. He didn't like what that would mean.

She shrugged. "Look at the book. It looks as though it rarely left Marcus's possession. And you said he always had it on him. And yet the police missed one of the most obvious places something would be, and when I arrive I stumble onto it that quickly?"

David had to agree it seemed pretty coincidental.

"And I don't believe in happenstance."

"Well, we agree on that," David murmured.

Surprised, she glanced up at him. "You think it was planted too?"

He blinked. He hadn't been thinking of that. "Well, yes. I mean I'm sure you know your job. And you're right. When you put it like that, it does sound suspicious."

"What were you talking about?"

He shrugged. "Oh. Well, I believe God orders our steps. And if I believe that, then I'm sure there's a reason you're here."

She groaned.

"You asked!" Amused by her reaction he resisted smiling. She was so prickly.

"I am quickly regretting it." She flipped the book back open.

"Tell me, sweet-gelina," he said when she glanced up sharply at him. He grinned, thinking that sounded like a good nickname for her.

"Yes?" she asked when he didn't continue.

"Tell me, why do you hate Christianity so much?"

"I don't hate Christianity. I just don't believe in it."

"Why is that?"

Her gaze concentrated on the book, and she flipped the pages one by one looking for something. "Christianity says to help your neighbor, to love your neighbor. That doesn't happen in real life. It's all about what I can do for God to make me look good, not what God wants me to do for people."

Oh yeah, she'd definitely been hurt. "So—?"

"Where is this?" She cut him off and he took the hint. She'd closed the subject, for now.

She handed him the book and he took the chance to allow his fingers to brush over her fingers again. He couldn't believe how soft her skin was compared to his. She pulled her hand away and slipped it into her back pocket.

He avoided a grin and studied the page in the book. He nodded. "You're right. This is a Wallabee entry."

"What's that?" she asked, her right hand pointing to a small mark near the entry.

"I don't know." He rubbed his finger over it. "The ink doesn't match what's on the page."

"My point. So we need to find this place mentioned here."

"You think someone marked this?"

Her features turned grim. "I'm almost certain."

For the first time since meeting this woman, David saw the professional in her and thought he wouldn't want to get on her wrong side.

He returned his gaze to the page. "I think this is a small bar down the street here." He pointed. "But don't you think we should call the authorities?"

She shook her head. "They want *me* for some reason."

"Exactly why we should call the authorities," David replied simply.

"Show me where it is." She started off.

David snagged her elbow and pointed the other way. "Down the alley here."

She didn't hesitate and headed down the alley.

At least she didn't have her pistol, he thought, following, and then considered picking up something along the way as a weapon, just in case.

The alleyway stank of rotting garbage. Flies buzzed. The noise of restaurants and the mercantile could be heard.

No one lay about in the alley, however, for which David was thankful.

He took the lead and stepped over garbage and around trash bins until he got two-thirds of the way down the alley. "This is it."

She looked up at the building.

It wasn't special, David thought. This was the main door that most people used. The other door let out into a field, so few walked there.

Angelina slipped in front of him and jiggled the door.

"They don't open until this evening."

"That's nice." She slipped out a pin of some sort from her back pocket and started jacking the lock.

David blinked. "I don't think that's a good idea."

Angelina sighed. She paused and turned to look at him. "You can leave anytime you want."

David frowned. "I wouldn't leave Marcus's sister out on the streets without help."

She gritted her teeth.

He couldn't help but smile once again. He'd smiled more in the last few hours than he had in the last year. She was quite an independent sort and her attitude amused him.

She glared at him then returned to her work. Within a minute, a quiet click told him she'd accomplished her purpose. She reached for her side and then sighed. "I need my pistol."

He pushed her aside and stepped in.

"Wait!" she hissed.

If someone was going in first, it wasn't going to be her, he thought.

She shoved at his back. "I'm the trained one."

He had to admit she was, but she was also a physically tiny woman. "I can handle all kinds of creatures," he informed her. "So don't you worry—"

She shoved him to the ground.

He grunted at the same time a gunshot sounded.

Reacting on instinct, he grabbed the woman

and pulled her toward him, an instinctive gesture of protection.

She let out a sharp breath.

"Let go of me, you oaf," she complained. "It was rigged. You tripped the wire."

He refused to release her. His heart beat staccato after what had just happened. "Tell me you're all right first. Tell me I'm all right," he added.

She shook her head. "We're both all right."

Her gaze met his in the dimly lit room and he realized he held her pinned to the floor. She was beautiful even when she was on the dusty, dirty floor. He wanted to hug her close and make sure she was okay.

Instead, he rolled away and let her go.

Instantly she sprang up and hurried forward.

All he could see was a shadow in the darkness, a shadow cast by the red emergency lights that shone from her break-in.

Her shadow went down.

He shot to his own feet. "Angie—!"

He nearly tripped as well when he came up against a solid object.

"Freeze!" she called out to him.

He did, not sure what he'd just kicked with his

toe, until she found the light switch and flipped the lights on.

At his feet lay a large man, at least as big as he was, in a dark suit, blood and matter oozing from a head wound. The sight shook him.

"Blue eyes."

David glanced to Angelina, her words halting any movements he would have made. She came up next to him. "What are you talking about?"

She toed the dead man's leg gently. "This was one of the men who kidnapped me. He had deep-blue eyes, the bluest I'd ever seen."

"We're alerting the authorities now," David said softly and crossed to the bar.

"I'm sure someone has already alerted them, if the silent alarm didn't get their attention," she said matter-of-factly.

He didn't care. "Well, I'm not used to finding dead bodies, sweetheart. I'm calling and making sure someone gets here quickly."

"Fine."

He paused. "Why aren't you arguing with me?"

She shrugged. "Whoever wanted me here made his point. He's telling me that he knows I'm here and he's planning to kill me. This man was killed because he failed to eliminate me."

David shook his head and dialed his cell phone. When it was picked up on the other end, he asked for Inspector Washburn. "We've found a dead body and it might have to do with the disappearance of Marcus," he said quietly into the phone.

"I'll be right there," the woman answered.

He gave directions and hung up.

Turning, he found Angelina leaning over the body. "Don't touch him," he warned.

"He wasn't killed here," Angelina told David.

He went forward, feeling a bit surreal. "How do you know?"

She pointed to the wound. "There's only a bit of blood. Had he been shot here, there'd be much more blood. And look how he's lying. Straight, as if he's been dragged. It doesn't look like he's fallen."

She glanced around the room. Nothing was out of place. Every booth was perfectly polished, cleaned. In the light she could see the floor had been mopped. Behind the bar the liquor was lined up in perfect order as if it had been straightened after closing. Her gaze sharpened. On the counter sat a half-full glass of beer. Next to it a bottle. She moved forward. Nothing was out of place—except this. Why? Someone had brought this body in here as a warning to them. But they wouldn't have stopped to have a drink. No, these guys were too professional for that. The empty bottle next to the glass was the key. It was set with the label facing them, deliberately, not by any accident. "Do you recognize the brand?" she asked David.

He nodded. "Sure. It's made about forty kilometers from here. The locals are real proud of it."

She nodded. That was the clue. That was where the unknown person wanted them to go. "Come on, let's go."

He blinked. "We can't leave yet. The inspector is on her way."

She frowned, remembering the dead body but torn over the fact that her brother was out there with a very dangerous individual who seemed intent on playing games with them. "I need to find my brother."

"And we need to do what's right."

Angelina let out an exasperated breath. Her hands went to her hips and then she turned and went to lean against the counter. "Very well."

David looked back at the man. He paced over next to her. Fisting his hands, trying to relieve the pent-up energy, he stretched his fingers out and fisted them again. Finally, he asked, "Do you wonder what his last thoughts were?"

"What?"

David glanced at Angelina. "The dead man. Do you wonder if he had regrets in his life? If he thought about eternity? Who was there to meet him when he died?"

She looked at him as though he were crazy. "No! He tried to kill me, and he's dead now."

David felt sorry for Angelina. "Everyone has a soul. Including this man."

Angelina's gaze slid away. "I know that," she finally said softly. Her shoulders dropped a bit and he realized she was hyped-up on adrenaline too. Now that she was coming down off the rush, she was careless and probably telling him more than she normally would. "That's one reason I'm not in the business anymore. But in this business, you can't think about that."

He nodded. It would be hard, he imagined, but still, he couldn't help but wonder.

"And if he hadn't been killed it would be because I'd been killed in the car."

Those words shook David. If this man had killed Angelina, he never would have met her.

Where would her death have taken her? He didn't want to think about that.

Actually, he had the overwhelming urge to go to her and hug her again.

But at that very moment, the police arrived.

He vowed that as soon as they were done here, he would take Angelina with him and make sure she was protected until he could convince her just how much she needed God—and him—and then they'd find her brother.

Yeah, that was definitely a plan. And he was going to make sure she listened to him.

Chapter Seven

The man had to be crazy if he thought he was going to boss her around like this. He was a *park ranger!* "I won't do it." She dug in her heels.

"Just come in for a moment. It's my flat and I really think we should discuss your plans."

She growled in frustration. "I'll call a cab to take me where I want to go if you won't take me," she argued.

"Okay, look." David frowned. "We need to eat. I need to get some supplies if you want to go trekking out to this brewery. How about you at least eat lunch with me and then we go?"

She studied him coolly. He didn't seem like a guy who gave in easily. After all, she'd told him she wanted to go to the brewery and they'd ended up at his apartment instead.

She didn't want to go into the apartment of a man who she really didn't know—yet for some reason, she felt she could trust David.

Still, she didn't like him not allowing her to do her job.

But she *was* hungry. "Just lunch and then promise me you'll let up?"

"I'll take you to the brewery myself."

She watched him closely for some sign of deceit and couldn't find any

Slowly, she nodded.

Getting out of the vehicle, she stretched. It'd only been twenty minutes to David's apartment yet her entire body ached. She was still experiencing jet lag. And she had to admit, finding Blue Eyes dead hadn't made her day.

Someone was trying to scare her away. And she didn't know whom.

But the clues and the dead man had been a very personal message.

She should know this person somehow.

But she didn't know anyone in Australia.

Still, murdered simply because the man had lost her suggested it was personal. The specific clue left just for her...the kidnapper had definitely targeted her for some reason.

Otherwise why wouldn't he have simply said, oh, well, kidnapping failed, we'll do whatever with her brother and leave her alone.

No, there was more to this than she could see right now.

And that worried her. It made her fear that she was missing something—something big. But what could it be?

"This way," David said and led Angelina through the maze of apartments to the one that was his.

He slipped a key into the door, pushed it open and stepped back to allow her entrance.

The apartment was very basic, but very different from what she was used to in America. The furniture reminded her of the late fifties or sixties, dark-brown and very masculine. A sofa and two chairs, a small coffee table clear of anything but a remote for the TV and a few magazines. The walls didn't have much on them: a scenic view of some Australian mountains and a photograph.

She walked over to it. "Family?" she asked.

"My mum and dad as well as my aunt, uncle and their children."

"And you, younger," she noted.

"Five years ago."

She nodded.

The sound of purring caused her to turn.

A calico cat circled David's feet.

"Hi there, sweetheart," David said and picked up the tiny cat. "How's my little sheila doing?"

He had a cat. She moved forward and reached up to scratch the cat behind the ears. "She's beautiful."

David smiled. "A cat lover eh?"

She smiled. "I don't have any pets, but if I did, it'd be a cat."

The cat's purring reached new volumes.

"She likes you," David murmured.

"Well, I like her."

"Smart cat."

Angelina blinked and glanced up at David. Was that attraction she saw in his eyes? And had he actually meant what she thought? She ignored it and turned to finish her inspection of the apartment.

A small dining area was to the left off the kitchen, and to the right was a bedroom.

David walked over to the kitchen and set the cat on the cabinet. Reaching under it, he opened a door and pulled out some food. "Hungry are you, sweetheart?" He stroked the cat as he filled her dish.

The cat began to eat.

"So, what's her name?"

"Sheila."

She didn't believe it.

He grinned. "I'm not real original."

"You're serious? You call her what would be the equivalent of 'girl' in America?"

He shrugged. "Well, she is a girl."

Angelina shook her head and then chuckled.

David filled Sheila's water dish and then turned to the fridge. "I have beef for sandwiches and some Vegemite."

"Vegemite…"

He pulled out the ingredients. "I can tell by your face you don't care for our necessary staple."

"It's too salty and…bland."

"What is it with the rest of the world? Only we Aussies truly appreciate it."

It was Angelina's turn to shrug. She walked over and fixed herself a sandwich but didn't sit.

David bowed his head, prayed and then bit into his sandwich even as he put the food back up.

"Oh, uh, you need a plate?" he asked.

"Actually, this is how I eat at home, on the go, so to speak."

He swallowed. "A sheila after my own heart, as you would say."

His words warmed her, and she didn't like that. And yet she did.

She went back to the living room and paced. David brought two sodas and handed her one.

"Why have they taken Marcus?" she asked after she swallowed. "What am I missing?"

He finished his sandwich and downed the rest of his soda before answering. "I wish I could help you. It has to do with the mission I'd bet."

She shook her head. After she'd swallowed, she continued, "Can't be. They wouldn't have bothered with me if it only had to do with the mission."

David nodded. "Then maybe you should look at the obvious."

Curiously, she looked at him. "And that is?"

"That it does have to do with your job and the president."

"But why kidnap Marcus? Unless what he was going to tell me was something they had to stop."

She set her bottle aside. "I need to call someone."

He nodded. "I have something I have to do in the other room."

As he left, she pulled out her cell phone. She called Josh. When he picked up she said, "It's me. How are you?"

"Busy. We have a hurricane in the Gulf."

Concerned, she sat down on the edge of the sofa. "Are you going to be okay?"

"Time will tell. How about you?" he asked, changing the subject.

She hesitated telling him anything with all he had going on back there. "Fine. Reception for my cell is spotty though. I'm in town right now, so I can actually reach you. Well look, I gotta go. Go take care of your problems. I'll call back in later."

She didn't wait for an answer but hung up. Opening her phone back up she waited for reception and then punched in a number she hadn't called in a long while. When it was picked up, she gave her old ID number and name. It must still have been valid because several clicks sounded and then her old boss came on the line. "Harding? Long time. Just why are you calling me now?" That was her boss, gruff and to the point. He'd never forgiven her for her past mistakes, nor for leaving.

"I'm Down Under and happen to have heard our old friend is coming down here soon."

He huffed. "He's no friend of yours." He let out a rough chuckle and his barb burned. "But yeah, he's going there, and I'd suggest you stay away." He chuckled again. "Seriously though. Why?"

"Any security problems?"

"Why?"

Of course, he wouldn't tell her. Frustrated with the tap dance she said bluntly, "My brother called me about something to do with my old job and now he's missing. Someone tried to kidnap me. I'm worried about our friend's safety."

"You're seeing ghosts behind every action, Harding. We have his security well in hand. You need to get over the fact he nearly got killed on your watch and let it go."

She shot to her feet in anger. "This isn't about that."

"Look, Harding, I'm sorry about your brother, but we've checked him out long before and no one he knows is a threat to the boss."

She bristled that they'd checked her brother out, but after what had happened with her, of course they would, or at least her boss, Jennings, would. "Fine. Still, though, if you hear anything…"

"We won't," he cut in sharply. "If you'd stayed, you'd be on the inside right now instead of on the outs. I'm sorry we lost you, Harding, but that's the way things go."

Arrogant jerk. "All right," she replied coolly. "If I hear anything I'll call."

"You do that. Now I have to go. Got some real stuff I need to take care of. Nice talking. Stop by sometime."

He hung up.

So did she. She'd been a fool to think he'd listen to her. She was the only bad mark on his record. He'd wanted her to stay, to make an example of her and she'd robbed him of that by resigning.

He'd called to check on her afterward, but in reality, it had been to do his best to make her miserable. She couldn't blame him in a way. He had feared for his own job when heads had started rolling over her actions.

The one man she'd trusted, the one she'd recruited into the business had betrayed her and all of them by nearly killing the president. And she hadn't been able to shoot him.

He'd gotten away.

And they'd never found him. They'd called him Scorpion. Stupid name but he'd been so careful with his steps, and then his sting, when it came, was big.

Of course, right now, she doubted anyone was worried about the past, what with trying to smooth over everything after losing their current vice president. The president had a huge job ahead of him to heal America. She really liked the president too. He was a good man and she was thankful that as vice president, he hadn't been killed on her watch.

She glanced around impatiently. Where was David?

She prowled through the living room and then toward the bedroom. Just as she was about to call out she heard a click—that she knew well. She reached for her pistol but it wasn't there.

Silently she cursed herself for trusting David.

She pushed the bedroom door open, determined to take him down before he could take her.

Standing across the room, a pistol in his hand, David had just finished loading. He turned at the sound of the door.

She rushed across the room toward him.

"Whoa!" he called out and pointed the gun toward the ceiling.

She hesitated before him in confusion. "What are you doing with a pistol?"

He still had it pointed at the ceiling, along with his other hand. His eyes were wide and startled. "You know, sweetheart, it's not safe to run at someone who's holding a loaded handgun."

"Give that to me," she ordered.

David lifted an eyebrow. "Okay," he said softly and handed it to her, confusing her all the more. "Just don't panic, all right?"

She took the gun, checked the chamber and then released the clip.

"What are you doing with this?" she demanded.

He still held his hands up, carefully watching her. "I only thought we might need some protection."

Embarrassed and angry, she picked up the clip and shoved it back in and then slipped it into the back of her pants. "And you weren't going to tell me?"

He shrugged.

She stepped back. "Oh, I get it. It's okay for you to have a handgun but not me?"

He tilted his head slightly and studied her.

"You thought I was going to use it on you, didn't you, sweetheart?"

"Stop calling me that."

Slowly, his hands came down and he stepped forward.

Angelina stepped back. She let out a breath. "Okay, yes, I did. I apologize. But, then, I still don't really know you."

Hurt actually flashed in his eyes before it disappeared. "I suppose that *is* true. But there is going to come a time, sweet—gelina, that you're simply going to have to trust me."

She wanted to, but at the same time… "I don't know if I can. My brother is missing."

He nodded. "And I showed up at just the right time. Would I have handed you the pistol if I'd intended to shoot you?"

She sighed.

When she didn't answer, his face went blank. "We should go."

"Answer me this first," Angelina asked, stopping David in his steps. "Why were you getting the pistol?"

"I'm qualified to use it, for one thing. And I think that your judgment is clouded. These clues are obviously a trap set for you."

"Yes, they are."

She'd actually surprised him. "If you believe that then why are you going to the brewery?"

Her eyes narrowed coolly. "Sometimes you have to spring the trap so you can get the cheese."

He looked at her as if she were crazy.

"It's all I have."

She turned to leave but David caught her by the arm. "I don't want you hurt," he said softly.

She paused and looked up to him. "And I don't want to be hurt, but I don't want my brother hurt either. I need to find out what he knows."

David didn't release her. "And you need to keep him safe."

She stared him down.

He finally said, "Like he should have kept you safe."

She felt every bit of color drain from her face. "If you aren't taking me, then I'm out of here."

She strode out of the bedroom and toward the front door. She heard nothing for a moment and then his sure steady strides as he came after her.

What type of man was this David?

He seemed so ordinary and yet stubbornly went with her to make sure she was okay. He wasn't from her world yet he had guns in the house and knew how to use them. He was quiet and loving to his cat and yet could look into the depths of her soul and read her mind.

He wasn't your everyday type of guy.

And he was a Christian.

At least she now understood a bit about him and knew she was going to have to guard her heart, because he had a way of cutting through all of her boundaries and seeing right in.

And she was going to make sure he didn't do it again—starting right now.

Chapter Eight

She had a way of getting right into his soul and turning him inside out, and he didn't like it. Especially when he realized he actually cared for this woman he'd only known a few hours. He had never believed in love at first sight, but, well, this little wombat had a way of making an impression. And it made him wonder if love at first sight was possible.

"Are you sure you don't want to call the inspector?" David asked now. They were less than five kilometers from the brewery and every instinct in him warned that they were racing headlong into a trap—and he knew that Angelina understood that as well.

"No. I want them to make their move."

"But if—" he started, only to see a flash out of the corner of his eye. "Watch out!"

A car shot out of nowhere and hit the side of the Rover. David braced himself with one hand and grabbed for Angelina with the other.

He felt his head connect with the window.

Someone jumped out of the other car.

"Take cover!" Angelina shouted.

His vision hadn't cleared, but he shoved his door open and bailed out, reaching for the inside leg of his boot where he'd stashed the other gun, the one Angelina hadn't seen.

"Out of the car, lady."

"Blue Eyes's friend," Angelina hissed.

He heard the words and scrambled to his knees, orienting himself to where everyone was.

Angelina was standing behind the car—how had she gotten there so fast?—and Blue Eyes's friend was on the other side of the vehicle that had hit them.

The car had been right there, in the brush near the roadway, hidden until they were close enough to ambush.

"Now come around here where I can see you."

"I don't think so."

"Do as I say."

"If you're planning to shoot, then I'd suggest you do it now. But then, you were expecting me to come out of the other side and so you don't have me where you'd planned."

There was silence.

"Where's the bloke?"

Angelina's voice was cool as she replied. "Unconscious. Wanna see?"

"Don't move!"

David quietly inched toward Angelina so he could see what was going on. She motioned away from where he was, while her other hand held a gun pointed at the man.

"You know, you really didn't plan well. If I were you, I would have brought two or three more men."

David quietly inched the other way.

The man laughed a nasty laugh. "I'm redeeming myself."

She nodded. "So, who shoots first?"

David was at a point now he could see the man from the side and Angelina's face nearly dead-on. Not a bit of expression showed. The man's gun was pointed at Angelina, but if her expression was to be believed, it was a day in the park, except for one tiny bead of sweat on her right temple.

She was sweating.

"I need to know who you've talked to since you've been here."

Angelina didn't blink. She replied promptly, guessing. "The president, and he knows your plan."

The man's finger twitched. He was going to shoot her.

Angelina didn't move.

David's eyes widened. He reared up. Pointing his pistol, he fired just a split second before the man's own gun went off. The impact was silent and fast. Blood bloomed on the man's chest as he turned toward David. His knees buckled and the gun tumbled from his loosened fingers to the ground as his body collapsed.

David jumped up.

Angelina's weapon still pointed at the man. Almost as an afterthought, she dropped it to her side and rushed toward the fallen man.

David thought he was going to be ill.

"Where's my brother!" Angelina demanded kicking the man's gun out of reach. Dropping to her knees, she grabbed at the injured would-be assassin's lapels. "Tell me!"

The man grinned, blood in his mouth. "As far from here as you are close to the brewery."

"I want an answer!" she demanded.

David reached into his pocket, grabbed a hankie. He dropped down to his knees next to the man and pushed the cloth against where the man bled from the chest. What had he done? There was blood everywhere. The man's face had turned gray. He was going to die. But he couldn't. David couldn't let him die. He had to save him.

Save him...in more ways than one. He put more pressure on the wound causing the man to hiss in pain. "Before you die, where is your heart with God?" David asked.

The man actually blinked.

"Not now!" Angelina croaked in disbelief.

David ignored her. "Ask for forgiveness. Tell Jesus. It's not too late."

The man stared at David and his features changed.

Angelina shoved back in next to David. "Out of the way, David. Where can I find my brother?"

"I can't be—forgiven," the man said, and then he gasped bitterly. His gaze was fixed on David, not Angelina. "I don't—want—it."

"You will," David said. "Please."

"David! Stop it!" Furious fire shot out of Angelina's eyes.

David didn't care. He wasn't going to be responsible for this man's soul. He couldn't be.

The man coughed and blood came out of his mouth. His eyes started to glaze over.

"You can."

"I—I—I'm…" The man shook his head. "I don't want to die."

"Ask. Don't go like this. Forgive me too," David whispered. "He loves you, even now. No one else might, but He does."

The man vaguely focused back on David. He stared for what seemed like an eternity and then his features changed. An almost peace-like state settled over him.

"Tell me! Where is my brother!" Angelina demanded again breaking into their rapport.

David leaned forward. "Jesus can be right here, right now for you. Just ask him. Trust him."

Angelina shoved at David as he leaned over the man. Low, against his ear, David whispered, "Please."

The man, his words more of a hiss than a voice, breathed out, "North, one hundred kilometers, old town, ranch…"

A last wisp of breath escaped and he wilted, dead.

"Answer me!" Angelina cried, not hearing what the man had said.

Then she realized the man was dead. She jumped up and stalked over to the car. She slammed her hand into it once, twice, then again and again.

David released the man. Physically ill, his head swam and his stomach churned.

He'd just taken a man's life. The most unnatural thing in the world to do, and he'd done it.

He fell over the man and prayed that God would have mercy on him and forgive him. Then he prayed for his own forgiveness.

He had never ever felt the way he did now.

"You idiot! How could you kill him? How could you do it?"

Adrenaline surged. David shot to his feet and turned toward Angelina. Her eyes blazed.

She came at him. Stopping in front of him, she slapped him and then hit him in the chest. She was strong. "How could you do it? How!"

He caught her hands and jerked her forward. "Because he was going to shoot you. And you froze!"

She erupted in rage and jerked against his hold. "No!"

He shifted to avoid her foot and then shifted again when she tried to throw him off. "Yes!"

And then he pulled her forward and kissed her.

She stiffened and jerked against him, but he didn't release her.

He deepened the kiss and then, finally let go of her.

She pulled back. "Why did you do that!"

She wiped her hand across her mouth as if she'd tasted something disgusting.

"Because you scared me to death and I thought I'd lost you!"

He turned and stomped off.

Angelina watched him go.

Her blood pounded in her ears. Her only source to her brother's whereabouts was dead, and her emotions were a mess. But there was one truth in everything that had just happened.

"You're right. I did freeze!" she shouted after David. He stopped on the side of the road. His hands on his hips, his head hung, he breathed as if a freight train had hit him. "And I froze the day the vice president was nearly killed. And I haven't been able to shoot anyone since then. And after that wild guess a minute ago, I now know that the man who is trying to kill me is after the president too."

David continued to breathe in harsh breaths while he stood with his back to her.

"And that was the first man you've ever killed," she said with sudden comprehension.

"Sorry, sweetheart, but I don't do this for a living."

Shame washed over her. On shaky legs, she went forward. She remembered the first person she'd killed. There had been two in her life. Five she'd shot, but two that she'd actually killed. It was a feeling she never forgot. They haunted her dreams at night. Because she'd frozen, this man had been forced to take a life for her.

She came up behind him and slowly lifted her hand. Tentatively she touched his back. "I'm sorry."

He shuddered and shook his head. "I shouldn't have kissed you."

"Adrenaline. Sometimes our hidden emotions come out during it."

He wouldn't turn and face her. She no longer focused on the fact that she'd lost the man who might lead her to her brother, but on David.

What had he done to her? Nothing but help her

from the very beginning. "You didn't ask to be involved. I chose you in desperation and it's led you to this."

She'd never really had to comfort someone like this before, and it was a new experience for her. How did people open themselves up to show they cared?

She stroked his back repeatedly, thinking that the motion comforted her so it must comfort him.

And it must have, for suddenly he turned around and pulled her into his arms. He trembled as he squeezed her. She found herself squeezing back, giving as good as she got.

"I thought I'd lost you. When I saw him ready to pull the trigger I thought, she's come this far and now she's going to die."

"I never have admitted that I froze. I left the agency because I couldn't admit that. Even my best friend back home doesn't know."

He ran his hands over her back, down her long hair, which hung in disarray about her. "I won't tell," he whispered. "I won't tell."

She started crying. Like an idiot. She was supposed to be comforting him, but she was the one crying. "I'm sorry," she whispered. "I'm so sorry."

"It's adrenaline, sweetgelina, and that you finally admitted something that you couldn't before."

"No it's not," she argued and continued to cry.

Amazingly enough, she felt moisture touching her forehead. "Yes, it is," he argued.

"You're strong-willed," she countered.

"Quiet but determined."

She chuckled, stepped back, and looked up at him.

His own tears were gone, as if they'd never been there. But she knew what she'd felt. He was so handsome, she thought, so protective, just what she imagined her knight in shining armor to be.

She reached out, cupped his cheek, and leaned forward to kiss him.

He accepted her kiss and returned it, his own hands cupping her cheeks.

She found she wasn't afraid of his kiss. She actually felt warmth from it.

He released her and stepped back, studying her.

"I have an idea where your brother is."

She blinked. "What?"

"The man whispered it as he was dying."

Angelina was having trouble digesting what

David said, her mind still reeling from the kiss and the stirred-up emotions.

"It's got to be another trap."

He slowly shook his head. "I think he found peace, Angelina. I think that was his way of showing it."

Angelina's features hardened. "Peace? He doesn't deserve peace. He was the enemy."

David reacted as if she'd slapped him. "No one deserves peace then, Angelina. God forgives us all if we'll accept it."

"He has to pay for what he's done."

David shook his head in disbelief. "No, Angelina. That's how it works."

"Then why do we have jails?"

She turned and headed back toward the car, pulling her cell phone out as she did.

David watched Angelina go, unable to believe what she had said. Angry, he went after her. "Yes, we have to pay. And we pay with wages from the sin. That man just paid with his life. Don't you think that's enough?"

"I'm not going to forgive him," Angelina told David flatly.

"Forgiveness is God's job. You can't dictate who he can and cannot forgive."

Storm Clouds

She sighed, ignoring his remark, and turned to face him. "I can't get a signal out here. Is there anywhere in this country you can get a signal?"

He resisted jerking the phone away from her. "Yes, God. God forgives. And eventually you'll have to forgive too. That's how it works. And I'll have to forgive that man."

"You? For what?"

"Well, I'm pretty steamed right now that he made me shoot him by trying to kill you."

Angelina stared at David as if she couldn't believe what he'd said. She then turned and jerked the door open. She got into the car and slammed the door.

"One, two, three..." He started counting as he walked around the car. "Four, five, six..." He opened the door. "God help me," he whispered. "Seven, eight, nine..."

"It doesn't help."

"What?" he asked, slamming his own door.

"Counting."

"Ten," he said succinctly.

She glanced askance at him.

"Eleven."

"I won't forgive him."

"If you don't, then God can't forgive you."

"Oh? So what happened to this all-loving God that everyone preaches about?"

"He loves you all right, sweetheart. He died for you. But He expects you to do your part, and that is to accept it and let go of the past."

"This has nothing to do with my past."

"Yes, it does. I don't know what, but this all boils down to your past. The job, everything, is connected to your anger at something that happened in your past. And until you let go of that, you aren't going to have peace."

"Who said I don't have peace?"

She was angry again. Her eyes flashed.

Somehow, that made him feel better. He relaxed. Maybe eleven was the right number. He knew it was God who made him feel better, not a number, but still.... He could hear the Holy Spirit inside him telling him to let it go for now, that He was working on Angelina's heart.

"Your eyes, sweetgelina," he said, using the nickname he'd coined for her. "Your eyes when you look deep enough."

She opened her mouth to say something, but her cell phone chirped.

She screamed in frustration. "*Now* it works! But thirty feet over there, it didn't! Hello!" she snapped into the line. Her eyes crossed. "Wrong number."

She snapped it closed. Flipping it back open, she dialed a lengthy number.

"Who are you calling?"

"Your inspector."

He sat back and waited, and, as he did, he began to pray, for her, for him, for the mess they were in and for the fact that he was attracted to this woman.

He was falling hard and fast, and this woman wasn't right with God. This didn't bode well.

But he knew God was in control and was going to take care of it. He'd just have to resist the urge to fix her and let the Holy Spirit do His work.

And in the meantime, he'd work at keeping his lips off hers.

Twice he'd kissed her, once in desperation and once when she'd initiated it. He didn't know why—well, yes he did. He cared for her and wanted to make sure she understood it.

Especially after he'd killed a man to save her.

Killed a man.

It was going to take a long time to recover from that—a long time indeed.

"She's on her way. And she asked us to stop piling up dead bodies in the meantime."

David glanced at her. Her words had brought a slight smile to her face. "I'm all for that. So, in the meantime, if we're to sit here, then what do you propose we should do?"

She glared at him.

He smiled. "I have the perfect idea."

Chapter Nine

Are you dead yet, Angelina? I doubt it.

How long will it take you to figure out that I sent you to the brewery to take care of my little problem for me? I'm sure he's dead now. The only question is did he wound you as well?

And did he talk? I doubt it. He was faithful to the bitter end, but just in case, I've moved your brother. He's way out in the bush. Way out. You won't find him now. I'm certain.

And in the meantime, while you're distracted with all of this, I'm actually able to do what I set out to do and this time, I won't fail.

You'll figure it out. Oh yes, you're too smart not to find him eventually, but by then, it'll be too late.

*Too late for him, for you, too late for everyone.
So come on, Angie, doll. Come find me. I'm
still waiting. Walk through the maze and see if
you've made the right turn this time.*

Chapter Ten

Angelina stretched as she got out of the Rover
and walked into the ranch house again. "Any
luck?" Steve asked coming forward. His gaze
was, of course, on David, not her.

David shook his head.

"We did find someone who could help us and
he told us where Marcus was, but by the time we
got there, he'd been moved. You were right, it was
a trap," David said turning to Angelina.

Angelina shook her head. "No. I think the man
gave us the right directions, but he didn't know
his boss's plans."

How was this man one step ahead of them?
"He's playing me like an amateur," she said in
frustration. "It's too coincidental what's happen-

ing. It's as if he knows what my moves are going to be."

"So what's behind it?" Steve asked.

Angelina stalked over to the sofa and dropped down on it. "I just don't know, but I should."

David came over and sat down. "Mind if I stay here tonight, Steve?"

"Of course not. You can have your old room or the guest house out by the dorms. I've made up Marcus's room for you, miss," Steve said as an aside to Angelina.

Angelina nodded. "Have you heard any word from the kidnappers?"

Steve shook his head. "Not a thing. Jake is awake but doesn't remember a thing. We're praying."

Pained at his reference to prayer, Angelina nonetheless nodded. "If you don't mind then, I'm going to shower and go to bed."

Steve nodded. "Uh, miss, there're some clothes in there for you. One of the misses at the school is your size and Ted got some donations."

She frowned. "Thank you."

She purposely didn't look at David as she left. She'd been with him too much today. She needed a break. By the time the inspector had arrived earlier, she'd been ready to shoot David herself. He'd wanted to play twenty questions while they waited.

She'd refused at first, but then her own curiosity had gotten the best of her and she'd agreed to play his stupid game.

She headed down the hall toward her room, remembering their questions and the ensuing answers.

He was an only child who'd grown up in Australia, and he felt he was called to preach. He had actually started working the streets lately, like her brother had done. He didn't come out and say it, but she thought he was considering joining the ministry as well.

And she'd inadvertently learned more about her brother. For one thing, he regretted sending her home.

That had been enough to shake her to her core. Could that really be true?

If so then why hadn't he called her?

She'd never told him about the physical abuse her uncle had ladeled out, but then, he probably had some idea. After all, her uncle had abused him, though he'd never touched her when he'd been there. And she'd never told him the ugly way her uncle had looked at her that had made her run—or what had happened when she'd returned that made her run away for good. She had never told her brother she'd been sexually abused—nor would she tell anyone, except the therapist. The shame had been and still was too much to bear at times. It certainly angered her. She hated her brother for letting it happen and yet blamed herself as well. She thought if she ever told anyone other than her therapist she would explode, so she'd tucked it away. But the situation with her brother forced it back to the surface and her mild attraction to David only made the memories more painful.

She had been tired, angry and confused by the time the inspector had arrived.

The inspector had interrogated them for a long time. They'd then traveled with Washburn and Roberts to where the dead man had said her brother was and had gone over the place with a fine-toothed comb.

Someone had been there. They'd found traces of blood.

She didn't even know if her brother was still alive.

Stepping into the shower, she allowed the

forceful stream to wash away the blood and dirt of the day and to ease the aching muscles. Once washed, she grabbed an old robe left for her and quickly donned it. "Is he alive?" she asked into the air. "Are you there, God? Everyone keeps talking about You. So tell me. If You're there, why has this happened? Where is my brother?"

She was angry with God, too. At least, her friend Josh would say that. She said she wasn't, but maybe she was. Maybe Josh had been right and she actually did believe in God and did care that He'd let all of this happen.

Pulling on a pair of shorts and T-shirt, she grabbed up her dirty clothes and went back to her brother's room.

She closed the door, checked the room thoroughly, and then glanced out the window to survey the surroundings.

This room had all kinds of mementos that reminded her of her brother.

She folded the sheets back and got into bed. When she fluffed the pillow, her fingers met a solid object. She lifted the pillow to see what was there.

It was a book.

Her brother's Bible.

How had the police missed that?

She laid it on the bedside table and stacked the pillows before crawling under the covers.

Picking up the book, she thought that this was the cause of all of her pain—the reason her brother had left her.

She started to put it back down, but found she couldn't. It was a connection to her brother and might contain a clue.

She stared at the tattered leather cover. It was actually damaged and worn in places, the leather rubbed down to smoothness where he had evidently held it so much. The *H* of *Holy* and the *le* of *Bible* were gone. The crackled pattern was evident only as a darker brown than the base leather.

Slowly she opened the front page and felt shock down to her toes. Inside, affixed with yellowing tape, was a picture of her and her brother from when she had been only seven years old.

It too looked worn and old, as if her brother had stroked it many times. Around it were newspaper and on-line articles, laminated and held in by more tape. They were all about her—her job, her graduation from college, a note about her joining the Secret Service. She lifted each one— fastened to the cover much like a clipboard of papers. And as she looked at all six she shook her head in disbelief.

Folded, but not taped in, was the account of the attempted assassination of the vice president and how security had neatly stopped it. What the story didn't tell was how one Secret Service agent had frozen and allowed the man to get away while another man had taken the bullet meant for the vice president.

She trembled with utter disbelief to find out her brother had been keeping tabs on her all of these years.

Why hadn't he contacted her?

Why did he care?

She hated him.

Fresh tears burned her eyes.

In anger, she flipped open the Bible looking for other clues to prove that what she'd seen didn't mean what she'd just deduced.

She wasn't prepared for what she saw.

"For as the heavens are higher than the earth, so are my ways higher than your ways, and my thoughts than your thoughts."

Déjà vu, she thought and shook her head. It was as if God was answering her with that verse. His thoughts were so far above her that she couldn't see the entire picture. She knew how that went. In the Secret Service, they withheld the entire picture, telling them only what they needed to know.

She didn't like that answer, however.

Slowly she thumbed through the other pages, allowing them to drop open wherever, and as she did, she found more and more verses underlined. And with different ones, she found her ice-encased heart slowly thawing.

And gradually her heavy eyelids found it harder and harder to stay open.

The sting on her hand caused her to jerk awake.

Her eyes flew open and she found Ted standing before her. She'd fallen asleep—but how long ago?

She stiffened then flew out of bed, the Bible sailing to the floor as she did. In a fighting stance, ready to take him out if he moved closer, she demanded, "What are you doing here!"

Ted blinked. "I'm sorry, miss. I was getting up for the morning and heard you having a bad dream. I tried to wake you."

She glanced down at the sting on her hand and noticed a welt.

"You had a scorpion on you."

Her gaze shot back up to Ted.

"I swatted it off and killed it." He pointed to the floor.

She looked down and, sure enough, there was a dead scorpion on the floor.

"What's going on?" David stood in the doorway, hair mussed, a crease running down one side of his face, but his eyes alert and gun in hand.

He was barefoot as he came into her room and slid the gun in the back of his jeans. "Ted?" he asked curiously studying the man. Ted was very close to David's age.

Ted's gaze darkened and he shrugged nonchalantly. "I heard her having a bad dream and came in to wake her. She had a scorpion on her hand." He glanced around again. "I gotta go. Frank'll be here soon, if he's not here already." Without another word, he headed out of the room.

David squatted down and studied the scorpion. "Not a deadly type," he mused.

"But it hurts like there's no tomorrow," she muttered under her breath. She dropped down to the edge of the bed and rubbed at her hand.

"Let me see." David took her hand and examined the growing welt. "Wait here a minute."

He left the room. Angelina crossed to the closet and pulled on a robe over her pajamas. She had to admit her hand hurt so much she couldn't concentrate much.

Had she been dreaming? Yes, she had, but…

"Let's put this on it," David said coming back into the room. He had a paste of some sort. Reaching for her hand, he turned it over and smoothed the salve onto the hurting wound. Surprised, she stood there and waited as the throbbing subsided to a bearable level.

He continued to hold her hand and study it. "Feeling better?"

His hand was rough and callused, used to hard work, and so much bigger than hers was. Much more masculine than even Josh's, she thought. "Uh-huh." The words were quiet in the room.

David finally released her hand and knelt down to study the scorpion again. "We don't see this type in these parts much. I'm surprised."

Immediately Angelina's thoughts about how handsome this big Aussie looked squatting there next to her fled. She dropped down next to him. "These aren't usually here?"

He glanced sideways. "What are you thinking?"

She searched around until she saw something

to pick up the scorpion with—a piece of paper under the bed.

"Watch it!" David jerked her back as another scorpion came crawling out from where she'd just been reaching. He grabbed a nearby shoe and smashed the nasty creature.

"What—" Angelina leaned down on her hands and knees to peer under the bed, and then jumped back. "At least a dozen are under there!"

David backpedaled, pulling Angelina up with him. "Steve!"

His voice could shout the house down.

Footsteps echoed as several people came running down the hall. Angelina watched as a scorpion caught the edge of the spread and started its path upward.

"What is it? Where did those come from?"

"That's what I'd like to know," David told the crowd.

"We don't have those here," Frank said curiously, studying them.

"Sure don't," a young lady standing in the doorway said. Dark-brown hair, a dust mop in her hand, she gripped it as though she was ready to do battle with any scorpions that came her way.

"Don't worry, Charlene, I can get rid of them,"

a blond man said, nodding to the maid. He wore gloves and had a hoe, having just come in from gardening.

"Better you than me, Jason," another gardener joked, taking the hoe from Jason. He removed his gloves and shoved them into his back pocket.

Angelina trembled, her anger building. David felt it and immediately turned his attention to her. "Get some clothes. We'll let the gardeners clean this up."

She walked across the room, watching as her bed now swarmed with scorpions. Gathering her clothes and shoes, she paused by the bed.

"What?"

She handed her things to David and knelt back down to look under the bed again. The muted throb in her hand told her just how much pain she would have been in had she not awakened when she did. Carefully studying the underside of the bed, she drew her own conclusions, then stood, took her clothes back and walked silently out of the room.

Chapter Eleven

David watched her go, not liking the look in her eyes.

Glancing to the gardeners, he asked. "Your names?"

"Jeffery and Jason, sir."

"See that one of you get these out of here please."

The men nodded.

"Lately this house has been full of action," Frank mused.

"And none of it to do with finances," Steve added.

"You're glad about that, I'm sure," Frank said to David.

David sighed. "I'm glad the financial end is

going so well. It does enable me to continue in the job I'm in."

Steve studied David. "And when are you going to give that up and help us in the mission? You're rich. You don't need the job, except to find yourself, and I think you've known who you are from the beginning."

David shot a look at Steve, ignoring his comment. "I'm not giving up this job until we get all of this mess straightened out."

Those around David sobered.

"Any word on Marcus?" David asked, watching where Angelina had disappeared into the bathroom.

Steve sighed. "I talked with Inspector Washburn this morning. Nothing new. They're following up all of the leads."

David nodded.

Steve turned to the people gathered in the hallway. "Back to work everyone."

Slowly they dispersed. David ran a hand down his face. "The longer we don't hear anything, the more likely it is we won't find him alive, isn't it?"

"I wouldn't say that," Ted argued.

David studied Ted.

"He's right," Frank said. "There's been no ransom demand so it's possible that someone is simply holding him for another reason." The implication was that obviously the kidnappers weren't after David's money, something David hadn't considered until Frank's remark.

Steve nodded, his features dark. "But more than likely, they've killed him."

David glanced sharply at the door where Angelina had disappeared. "I won't believe that. We need Marcus."

"God will decide who we need and when," Steve said wisely. "And though I refuse to accept that Marcus isn't coming back, I think it's a possibility, and if it happens, well then, we have to trust that God will see to His ministry that He called Marcus and me to."

David sighed. He didn't want to think about the ongoing nightmare of his missing friend. "Since we're up can someone fix breakfast?"

Steve nodded. "We sure will. Will you be all right seeing to our missus?"

David nodded.

Steve and the others left. David slipped back into his room, washed up, and pulled on his boots. Just as he was buckling his belt, he heard the bathroom door open.

Angelina saw him as he stepped out of his room. He crooked a finger and she strode down the hall, once again in control and in charge. She walked past him into his room, and, with only a quick glance around, she didn't stop until she reached his window overlooking the front entrance. He thought about picking up his clothes from the night before, then shrugged, knowing that in her one look she'd catalogued everything in his room and had already seen his discarded outfit tossed on the floor.

He crossed to the dresser and began packing his pockets with his wallet and other items. "Tell me what you're thinking," he said looking in the mirror at her back.

"Someone put those scorpions in my room."

"I deduced that." He picked up his comb and quickly ran it through his hair.

"There was a jar with a lid balanced barely on top of it, just enough for the scorpions to find their way out."

"But why?" David asked. She turned and met his gaze in the mirror and David sucked in a breath at the steely look in her eyes.

"Someone is toying with me, and I think I know who."

He finished combing his hair, slipped his comb

in his back pocket and turned. "Well?" he said
when she didn't continue.

She moved away from the window and
dropped into one of the two chairs by a small
table where he'd studied his Bible last night. She
saw the Bible, picked it up, and flipped through
it before dropping it back to the table. "The Scorpion."

He looked blankly at her. He had no idea what
she meant. She sighed. "Sit."

His lips quirked. There was that dominant per-
sonality of hers. Still, he sidled over to the chair
and dropped down into it. Leaning forward, his
hands draped casually between his knees, he said,
"Continue."

"It's got to be him."

He held up a hand. "Can you start at the beginning for this poor uneducated Australian?"

She made a face at him and he grinned, realizing he'd scored a point with her. "I apologize."
Her gaze slid past his and she said, "Remember
when I confessed that I hadn't been able to shoot
the man who'd tried to kill the vice president?"

"Your current president."

She nodded. "I had recruited him to the Secret
Service. I'd met him and thought he was the per-

fect type for our business. Young, serious-minded, very patriotic, very into the political scene, just like I'd become. And he flew through the training. What I didn't realize, and neither did our superiors, is that he had an agenda of his own."

"Really." David frowned, wondering where this was going.

"Quantum encryption was just starting to become a hot topic and he had a vested interest in such things. And unbeknownst to any of us, he'd gotten heavily involved in the research end of it."

David was missing something here. "Quantum encryption?" he asked.

Angelina explained. "It's cutting edge, involving a type of LED that fires photons in a single steady stream—the photons relay the numeric keys used to code and read secret material. They are incredibly sensitive, and any disruption changes their behavior and alerts the people sending the information. I don't really understand the physics behind it, but it's virtually impossible to break the encryption. It's the future.

"Our vice president is heavily against such things, or rather, was at the time, and it was felt he could influence the president and was influencing him on such matters."

"So your friend tried to assassinate him?"

"And I froze."

"But why?" David asked and suddenly he knew. "You were involved with him."

The only sign he'd scored was the slight tightening of her mouth.

"He had me fooled. And another Secret Service agent nearly lost his life because of me."

David worked hard to keep all emotion off his face. "So you think he's toying with you now?"

She gave a short nod. "It would be just like Hank. He enjoyed mind games—immensely."

"And you call him the Scorpion?"

She nodded. "Because of his mind games. He was good at them and was very careful until the sting came."

"So what do you think he's up to?"

"He dropped off the face of the earth after trying to kill the vice president. We traced his accounts, but they'd been emptied and all hints of his whereabouts were gone. We never were able to find him again. We did hear there was someone still in the business a few years ago, financing the research of weapons so tiny, they can get past the best security, but no one has been able to trace where he was. I had wondered then, if it was Scorpion but it's been so long."

"Why would he worry about that? Why not find something else to invest in?"

"Because this very well could be the future if it's not blocked. We're talking revolutionizing warfare. Think about it. Whoever controls quantum encryption could control the future. But they need the technology to get it done."

"And your president is coming here to talk about a crackdown on this with our leaders. Which has something to do with that?"

She nodded again. "The encryption they're working on. Whoever controls that could send in robotic weapons that no one could stop, or they could use it on their computers and it would be virtually impossible for anyone to hack. America is determined this type of cryptology be kept with us and our weapons. And we're getting ready to appoint some new judges in our country who may very well rule on this in the future…this is too many coincidences."

"How so?"

"It's something Americans, and other scientists, have been working on for years. If we could develop a quantum encryption program that works on the quantum level, we would have an encryption that would be more powerful than enigma was in the second World War."

David nodded.

"This encryption could be put into robotic weapons that no one could stop. They wouldn't be able to be reprogrammed for enemy use. We would hold the codes. And we've been working on weapons so small and precise…" She trailed off, not willing to say anymore.

"Why would he tell you though, if he is going after your president?"

"He's arrogant. I'm positive my brother found out something and called me. Scorpion had him snatched. When he found out I was on my way, he figured if he can't get rid of me, then he can lead me on a merry chase while he goes about whatever it is he's planning."

"We need to call someone."

"Yes. And we need to find my brother."

"But what about your president?"

Angelina stood. "I'll call someone and put a bug in their ear, but it won't do much good if we can't figure out what Scorpion is up to. We need to find Marcus and learn what he knows."

"Maybe you should suggest your president not come here."

Angelina looked askance. "First off, my former boss would rather listen to a rat than listen to me after what happened, and secondly our president would never cancel his trip.

"Our president can't afford to look weak after the near scandal. He'll be here, no matter what."

"Americans," David muttered.

Angelina smiled. "And I'm very proud to be one."

David chuckled.

She pulled out her cell and walked toward the window. She checked it for a signal and then dialed a number. David watched her. She was graceful, lithe, beautiful. And brave. He thought of it as rashness sometimes, but it really wasn't. She'd had a hard life and yet didn't let that get her down.

He heard her say her name and some numbers into the phone and then wait.

He leaned back in his chair. He wondered just what she'd seen in her job.

"Tell him it's important. Scorpion may be here in Australia."

Having trouble getting through to her boss? He frowned.

"Yes, I think so."

She turned from the window and paced, her eyes set in steely determination. She was so focused, so tuned in on the job at hand. He could see why she'd ended up protecting her government. Whatever she did, she did it with everything inside her. He wondered if she fell in love like that—with everything, and that's why that Hank fella had been able to pull one over on her.

"Don't give me that. We don't have time—" She paused. "Your head is so far in the clouds that you can't even hear what I'm saying, can you?"

Oops. Not a good thing to say to a former boss, David thought.

"Well I'm not your employee any more now, am I? So you can't fire me for my words. And I'm telling you, if you don't check this out, you're a fool."

She turned and snapped her phone closed. "Totally rejected what I said and hung up on me."

He chuckled. "Well, you are a bit no-nonsense."

She sighed. "He gets under my skin. He's so arrogant. Anything I say he dismisses. Maybe Wheaton, who answered, will take what I said seriously."

David pushed up out of his chair and came forward. He grabbed her shoulders. "Take a deep breath and calm down."

Her gaze shot to his. "I am calm."

"You look like you didn't sleep well last night."

She shrugged.

"Ted said you were having a dream?"

She headed toward the door to leave his room. "Yeah. And is it normal here for people simply to walk into a room unannounced?"

"Not really," he said following her. "Especially not a male walking into a female's room. It must have been some dream."

"A nightmare," she said as she strode through the hallway.

"Your brother?" he asked, compassion welling in his heart.

"My uncle," she said shortly and stepped into the main room.

Her uncle? He faltered, wondering what type of nightmare she might have about her uncle.

"Breakfast is ready," Steve said, walking out of the dining room. "I've already eaten. Why don't you two help yourself?"

David nodded then turned to Angelina. "You need to eat before you hit the trail."

He could tell Angelina was torn. Finally, she turned and went into the dining area.

"Look. Jake tried to cook some American things," David said, seeing the grits.

For the first time Angelina slowed down. "That was really thoughtful."

She went forward and seated herself.

David walked around the table and sat down as well. He said a quiet prayer and then started serving himself a plate of food.

"I found my brother's Bible last night," Angelina said as she served up her own food.

"Really?"

"He read it a lot." She buttered a piece of toast and took a bite.

"All the time."

"He was never like that at home, until his last year there."

David wanted to tread carefully. "Marcus didn't talk much about his past."

"I'm not surprised. We didn't have the best childhood."

"You lived with your uncle?" he asked carefully as he spread some Vegemite on his toast.

She wrinkled her nose at his choice of condiment and then took a spoon and proceeded to scoop some flesh out of the kiwi on her plate. "We did. He had custody after our parents died."

"I'm sorry."

She shrugged. "I was only five. I barely remember them. Things like a smell or a certain story our mom used to read to us, that's about all I can remember."

What must it have been like for a young girl not to have a mum? "I miss my own parents still."

"I learned early it's up to you to get along in life. So did Marcus."

"How did he get saved?" David asked curiously. He took a swig of hot tea.

Angelina added some water to her tea, diluting it until it was a golden color. He thought that very odd, and Marcus had always done the same thing. "One of his friends at school. He came home with a Bible. The kid had actually given it to him. I recognized it in his bedroom immediately. It's the same one."

David hadn't known that. "Marcus became very inward after that, always spending time in his room, reading. My uncle didn't care as long as he had someone to do the work."

Ah ha, David thought. "And then Marcus went to some meeting and came home saying he had to go to Australia. I didn't understand why at the time. I still don't. If he wanted to save people, we have plenty of people in America who need help."

Bitterness had crept into her voice. He'd definitely found why she was the way she was. Her brother had left her with an uncle who'd used her as menial labor.

"And when I came to live with him, he made me go back home because I wasn't eighteen yet."

She'd run away from home and David had sent her back.

"His Bible had always come first, so I left it that way. I stopped contacting him."

"He didn't stop thinking about you. He mentioned a few times how he should have brought you over and not left you there, but that you'd turned out all right and he was proud of you."

She sipped her tea and then set it aside. "I found articles about me in his Bible."

Bitterness and confusion warred in her voice. "I don't understand why, when he sent me back into that nightmare, he could actually have thought he cared about me. It had to be guilt that made him follow my career."

David sat a bit straighter. "Nightmare?" he asked.

Her lips twisted. "Didn't you ever wonder why Marcus never talked about his childhood?"

David suddenly saw what was coming. He didn't want to, but he'd heard stories here from young men and women who'd been saved and come to live with them. He braced himself.

Angelina patted at her lips with the napkin and then looked David straight in the eye. "Our uncle did his best to kill us both before we were eighteen. And my brother, knowing that, sent me right back to him, where I had to face even worse than he could have imagined."

She tossed her napkin on the table, stood and strode out of the room.

David watched her go and wondered just how much worse it could be. He tossed his own napkin on the table and vowed he was going to find out.

Chapter Twelve

Well, you know now who it is. I have no doubt. And I know our former boss. He won't listen to a word you say. How frustrated are you, Angelina? How used are you feeling now? You were always so vulnerable with me. I could always lead you where I wanted you to go. And you had no idea, did you?

Well, Angie, doll, I already know your next move, and I'm prepared. The maze is quickly coming to an end, the jaws of the trap are opened and waiting for you to walk into them.

So come on. You've set everything in motion for me that I needed and now I only need one more thing—I need to find out exactly what the president knows about me and my past, and if you ever found out the truth as well. So take that next step.

I'll be waiting. I'll be ready.

And you'll be dead.

Chapter Thirteen

"This is the place?" Angelina looked around.
They'd had to wait until evening, as the tiny disco
would be empty in the daytime. She'd had time
to walk all over the grounds, see just what Marcus had accomplished, and hear so much from so
many people.

And it had given her time to calm down after
talking with David about her uncle. She hadn't
told David everything, but she'd told him enough
that she had been keyed up and needed to do
something to release her pent-up energy.

She still didn't like talking about her past.

"Ready to go in?"

She glanced again at the dingy front of the

building in Fleting, the neon sign on top that flashed. "I hope this works out."

"Are you sure this is the place you want to be?"

She nodded. She'd struck pay dirt by canvassing the compound. Some of the people from campus had been in Fleting the night she'd gotten the call from Marcus and they'd remembered seeing Marcus in Fleting at this small disco. "A kid was certain about seeing Marcus in here just before he was taken. Scorpion was probably trying to lead me in another direction and I hope to catch him off guard by coming here instead. Maybe I can discover just what Marcus found out here that led him to call me." She shoved her long hair back over her shoulder and with a nod to David grabbed the door.

Together they walked into the smoke-filled din of heat and noise. Old-time music from the early eighties blared from loud speakers and a huge glitter-ball hung in the middle of a dance stage, turning, causing the colored lights to flash off its metallic squares. "Wow!" Angelina looked around. "I feel like I've stepped back into the seventies or eighties."

David touched her elbow to guide her toward

two stools around a small table. "Yeah, looks like fun, huh?"

His voice said just the opposite.

She glanced at him as she climbed up on the stool and shifted to get comfortable under an air vent. "Sounds like you used to live this scene?"

He nodded. "Very much so. And I wonder now what I saw in it. No fun going out getting drunk, waking up the next morning with a hangover." He shuddered. "I guess I was filling a space that was empty. Besides, I have more fun now than I ever did before."

A man came over to take their order. "Soda," Angelina said and glanced back out to the dance floor. As if from a distance, she heard David order a nonalcoholic drink of his own. Her focus was elsewhere, she was there to observe and to note if anyone seemed shocked by her appearance there. She was watching for anything out of the ordinary.

"Hey, baby, you're not from here, are you?" She smiled at the man who walked up and leaned forward.

"Back off," David said.

"Hey sorry, mate," the man added and continued on his path around the room.

"I'm capable of handling myself," Angelina told David.

He shrugged.

"And I *am* here to mingle and see what I can find out."

"I don't know that this is a good idea," David told her.

She studied him. "What's the matter?"

"I can't help but be worried about you."

She realized it was because he cared. That warmed her. She reluctantly admitted she was drawn to him, but that distracted her when she should be concentrating on her brother.

"What's taking our drinks so long?" she asked.

He allowed the subject change. "I don't know. Want me to check?" he asked.

She shook her head. "I used to go to places like this a lot a long time ago. When I was a bit wilder."

"What did you find in them?" David asked more softly as the music died down and a slower, quieter ballad began to play.

Their drinks arrived and she took a sip of the carbonated soda. "Escape from reality."

She scanned the crowds, watching as two by two people paired up to dance. "It was fun in a way," she added.

"But in the end, you were still alone and still had to face the ghosts."

Angelina glanced at David. "Yeah. So I decided to go into a business that would focus that energy."

"The Secret Service."

Angelina nodded. David asked her questions about it, she asked him about his work, and slowly an hour passed. As they sat there, the old emptiness of her past life filled her. She remembered the days of trying to fill every waking moment with this so as not to remember her past. Until she'd gone to work for Josh. He'd told her that God could fill that emptiness, but she'd never believed it, not until she'd come down here to Australia. Last night, reading her brother's Bible, she'd actually felt a temporary peace. She wondered if it was actually possible to experience that on a more permanent basis.

She hadn't ever known peace, except around her boss, and in a strange way, around David as well. He was a good man, the type of man she could trust and respect. And though he was easygoing, he was smart, intelligent and a man she could give her heart to. They ordered a second and then a third soda. And by the time they ordered the third, she'd decided tonight had been a waste in trying to find her brother. "I think this is a dead end," Angelina said as the waiter went to get their drinks.

"Always is in places like this."

"I meant as far as finding a clue as to what is really going on."

"Do you have any ideas you might want to share?" David asked.

Angelina sighed, her gaze scanning the room. "I thought coming here might pay off, show me someone or something that my brother might have seen."

"Like what?" David asked. "Remember, I'm not in this type of business."

Well, they'd gone an hour, Angelina thought as her gaze scanned the room again. Something niggled at her as she went back to where she'd just glanced. People still danced, but many were drunk by now, having overimbibed. Some were getting overly friendly with their dates while others were finally working up the courage to approach those who weren't hooked up yet.

Oh, it was all so familiar and so empty.

Their third round of drinks arrived.

Angelina took a sip.

"So, when will you be ready to admit that what you've been missing is God?"

"I don't know," she said absently, scanning the room as more and more she felt she was not seeing something.

David obviously took her noncommittal words as a good sign because he continued. "We all are hurt, have pain, but we have to forgive that and accept that God forgives us and them as well."

Her gaze snapped to his. "I don't have to forgive," she said lightly, though she felt anything but. He kept going back to forgiveness. She would not forgive her brother. How could she? She fanned herself thinking it was too warm in this small room. Forgiveness was overrated as far as she was concerned.

"You will, eventually."

She simply shook her head and drank some more of her soda.

"I've got to find my brother," she whispered, low, changing the subject.

"We will," David assured her.

Tension bowed Angelina's spine. David reached out and ran a hand down her back. "Try to relax."

She shook her head. "Something isn't right here."

Surprised, David paused in rubbing her back. "What do you mean?"

The darkness in the room was contrasted by the bright flashing lights that spun and flashed off the large round globe. Smoke choked Angelina and she wished, for once, she was out of here. "I hated this work. I was glad it was over."

David didn't comment.

"What do you see in here?" she asked.

"I see that you're about to climb the wall," David quipped. She shook her head, and he said, seriously, "I see a lot of people mingling, looking for some fun."

"But what else? I'm missing something. My skin is crawling."

Her gaze went back over to the other side of the room. David must have noticed that she wasn't really paying attention to him because he paused. "What's up?"

Frowning, she said, "I just don't know. Something caught my attention, but I can't figure out what it was."

Angelina was distracted as she saw David's gaze comb the room. He tried to follow Angelina's example and sip on his drink as if nothing was amiss. She noted the fine sheen of sweat across his brow as he tried to act so relaxed.

"It's dark in here," David muttered.

"This side of life is. It's always dark when you're working on the other side of the law."

He realized she wasn't talking about the lighting but the soul. "Your thoughts are dark as well."

"My brother is out there suffering. I have to find him."

"Hey that's funny. There's our gardener," David suddenly said, his gaze sharpening.

"Where?" Angelina's gaze followed David's across to the spot he was focused on. Sure enough, there was the gardener in the shadows. "That's it. That's what I saw. What would a Christian gardener be doing in here?"

"Witnessing," David replied, as if it were a foregone conclusion, "Though I don't know why he wouldn't have come up and said hi if he's been here very long."

Angelina shook her head. "But he's not, witnessing that is. He blends in. Study his clothes, David, and the look on his face."

"What?"

She sighed. "He's dressed like everyone else."

"Well, that's not a crime."

"No, but he's not awkward in his clothes. Or that he's in here. I've known enough Christians in my life to know that in a place like this they stick out like a sore thumb."

"Yeah, I suppose. I can remember even though Marcus looked totally relaxed he did stand out from everyone else."

Angelina nodded. "Just like you do in here. But not Jason. He's at ease, and he blends too naturally."

"I think you're right," David said slowly.

"You're not used to deceit. However, I am and I may have found what I was looking for." She stood.

Jason saw her stand. He leaned forward toward a dark-haired man dressed in black jeans and a black shirt to whom he'd been speaking, and then turned toward the back of the room. "He's running," Angelina said.

"Jason is a new employee," David said and stood as well. "I haven't seen him at the mission before."

Angelina tripped. "Whoa," David said and caught her.

"It's too crowded in here. I don't want him to

get away," she muttered and started pushing through the people.

"Wait up, sweetgelina," she heard from behind her.

But she wasn't going to. David was tall enough that he could see her easily and not lose sight of her. She felt the warmth of David's pistol in her boot and itched to draw it, but she knew that would cause a panic.

Weaving in and out of the people, she found herself becoming disoriented. What was going on?

She reached up and wiped the perspiration from her brow. The people around her stank of perfumes, cologne and sweat.

A hand grabbed her arm. "Steady there," David said and guided her toward the other side.

"It's too warm in here," she muttered.

"Yeah, I'm noticing that."

The crowd thinned and she caught sight of the long hallway and the exit door swinging shut. "He's getting away."

She reached down and pulled her pistol, sticking close to David's side so the pistol stayed hidden.

"Are you crazy?" he asked, and inadvertently shoved her up against the wall.

Her gaze shot to his and things fell into place. Her glance went behind her and then back in front of her. "How far to the car?" she asked.

"Not far. We'd have to go back through the crowd."

She shook her head. Nausea roiled. "Can't. We're going to have to go this way."

David wiped at his brow. "It's awfully hot."

She forced herself down the hallway, watching for anyone who might be waiting for them. "No, David, it's not. I want you to go in the bathroom and wait for me."

David's gaze sharpened on her and she sighed. "Just do it and don't argue," she shot out before he could say anything.

"I don't think—"

"Good. Don't think. Just do what I say." She grabbed his arm and shoved at him. "Please."

"Someone slipped something in our drinks," he concluded.

Her face tightened. "I wasn't paying enough attention to our surroundings. I hadn't expected that."

Dizziness swept her. She shoved the gun at David and reached for her cell phone. "We need help now."

She turned and actually staggered against the

wall. Flipping open the phone she found, of course, no signal. "Idiot town. No signal."

David shoved the pistol in his belt and grabbed at Angelina. He looked one way, then the other and then found the nearest unlocked door.

"What are you doing?" Her world spun with each step.

"Trying to buy us some time."

Angelina glanced around the room. "A phone. An office," she muttered.

David staggered as he turned and locked the door.

Angelina started forward and met carpet instead as she went down, face first, to the ground. "Ow," she muttered wincing at the hard fabric that brushed against her face. It smelled of dirt and needed a vacuum.

She was scared. This was the first time she'd ever been stupid enough not to watch her drinks and end up poisoned. She grunted and tried to shove herself up onto her hands and knees, but found herself paralyzed. Terrified and angry she did something she'd never thought to do. "David… help…me…please…."

She saw his feet stagger past her. "Hang on, sweetheart. I'll get to the phone."

Tears of frustration filled her as she felt her body going numb. Perfectly still, she knelt there, but her entire world spun. She heard a loud sound but couldn't look up to see what it was. Everything was going dark. "Da-a-a-vid!"

Darkness engulfed her with his name on her lips.

Chapter Fourteen

"You are an imbecile."

"Hey mate, no need for name-calling, there."

"What possessed you to bring them here?"

"They showed up at the club and saw me."

Angelina heard the voices as if through a tunnel, far away, coming to her distorted, but enough that she could follow the conversation as she worked hard to wake up.

"They would have had no idea who you were had you not blown your cover, Jason. I'm very disappointed in you."

Angelina heard a popping sound and a thud. Vaguely she recognized it as a gunshot.

Please help me wake up, she thought to herself and then realized that it was more of a prayer than anything else. Where was David? Where had Jason taken them?

Things weren't as dark as they'd been minutes before. Instead of pitch-black, it was more twilight to her eyes. She attempted to assess her situation. Her feet felt the floor beneath her though she couldn't move them. They were bound to something solid—a chair. She sat in a chair. Something held her in it—a rope, she realized. She could feel the thick bands around her waist cutting into her tightly, scratching through her ripped shirt.

Her hands were stretched tightly behind her, bound together by more rope. And her hair hung loose about her, brushing her thighs as her head hung forward. It was almost impossible to lift her shoulders back against the chair. Whatever drug they had used still affected her enough that her body felt like a lead weight.

Slowly her jeans-clad legs came into focus, no longer a murky gray but still very dark.

She smelled blood in the dank dusty room. Perhaps a basement of a home. The floor beneath her feet was cement though it was hard to see. She could see the reflection of a small light in the distance. The sound of a door and footsteps echoed from the other side of the room.

"Awake yet, my dear?"

She knew that voice. Where did she know it from?

"I can tell you are."

An Australian accent, but not exactly. Feet came into view. Dress shoes covered in dust.

Someone roughly grabbed her hair and pulled her head back and she came face to face with Frank, the accountant.

"You?" Confused, she stared into his eyes and then realized his eyes weren't blue at all, but green, a very familiar green. A green that she used to love to stare into years ago.

"Scorpion," she said flatly.

Frank laughed and released her hair. "Indeed, Angie, doll. How nice of you to finally remember, though after plastic surgery it might be hard to recognize me." He leaned down and brushed his lips against her cheek.

She jerked away.

"Aw, I'm disappointed," he mocked and stood up. "After being separated so long, I thought you'd at least welcome me back. Is it the cheekbones? The nose? The chin? Or maybe that I've bulked up some that you don't like."

She hated him and had no qualms about admitting it. "I'd rather welcome a snake back than you."

He laughed. "I see you haven't changed a bit, Angie doll."

"Other than learning not to trust anyone in the business," she retorted.

He tsked and paced over to a table in the dark drab room. "It's not about trusting others, my dear, but about learning to set your sights on a goal and go after it."

His voice had changed, deepened some over the years and his different accent made it even more odd, but still, how had she not known him? The movements in his body, now that she knew who he was, gave him away. The way he tilted his head as he waited for an answer...

"Like you did the day you tried to shoot the vice president?"

He nodded. "About that..." He reached behind him, picked up an old-fashioned metal flashlight, and tapped it in his hand. "It is rather dark in here. I prefer to carry a flashlight here. Unfortunately, I have to apologize for the accommodations, as I wasn't expecting you for another two days. My former employee brought you in too soon."

He motioned and flipped on the light toward a corner where she saw Jason lying in a pool of blood.

She refused to react. "Where is my brother? Where is David?"

"They're around. However, I have some questions I'd like to ask you."

"You've got to be kidding." She managed to look down her nose at him even though he stood and she sat.

He backhanded her with the flashlight.

Pain exploded behind her eyes and she tasted blood. Lights flashed and she thought for a brief moment that she would lose consciousness again. She sucked in a breath and threw her head back, working to focus back on Scorpion. His hand flashed again and a square gold ring hit her as his hand came back across her face. Pain, right under her eye from that ring, tore at her skin. She saw stars.

"You've never been on the receiving end of my wrath, Angie doll, so don't force it now. I'm an expert in my field." He casually walked to one side of her.

Angelina licked her lip and glanced up sideways at him, watching the flashlight, the ring, the way they moved so gracefully as he caressed the metal tube as if considering how to use it next. "And what is that?"

He came back toward her. "For years I've brokered deals between governments for various things. Why do you think I joined the Secret Service?"

She simply stared as he ambled back into her view and then away again.

"So, you hadn't figured it out. My dear, you didn't recruit me. I recruited you. You were set up from day one to approach me."

Angelina's mind whirled. She'd been a fool back then, running hard from her uncle when she'd joined the Secret Service and looking for love from someone—anyone after what had happened.

Oh, it made sense now, how he'd been there for her.

"No comment?"

He paced around behind her and grabbed her by the hair, jerking her head back. Forcing a kiss on her, he caressed her cheek with his other hand, his long fingers running over her bruised skin, the cold feel of his ring caressing her cheek. She jerked and he held on just a moment longer before he let her hair go.

"We knew all about your uncle, all about your brother. You see, we needed someone close to the president because he was disrupting the flow of our money, thanks to his vice president. We weren't sure if we were going to have to do something about him or not, so I was sent in. And thanks to the assassination attempt on him, the winds changed, for a while that is. You see, we have people near all the major powers."

"Who is we?" she asked, unable to resist. She felt on a precipice, about to step over. Something about this man had eluded her for so long and she was about to find out what, if she was careful.

He grinned. "We're the power behind the world economy. That's enough for you to know. We've been around for many years and I am one of many. No, I'm not one of the top echelon, but I do help make sure they're able to carry out what they need to do, even if it means governments being toppled, presidents being assassinated... you understand."

"The tribunary commission." She'd heard rumors of what he was talking about but no one really believed they existed.

"Very good."

The tribunary commission was a fictional—or

so she'd thought until that moment—group of men and women who manipulated the world economy and governments. They were so secret that no one knew if they really existed or not. Her brother had chatted about the concept once during a Bible discussion. "I'd think weapons too small for someone like that."

She'd had no idea what she had stumbled into until now. She wondered if her brother was even alive after discovering just for whom Scorpion worked.

"So, you've figured out that much. But it's more the quantum end instead of the robotics and such. We leave the weapons for the terrorists." He nodded. "Now the question is, just how much have you told our former boss, Jennings, and how much does the president know?"

Angelina's lips tightened.

"Oh, you will tell me, Angie, doll. I will know, and then when I'm done with our little plan, you'll be eliminated."

He walked toward her. Angelina thought of David and Marcus and hoped they were able to escape.

Chapter Fifteen

David heard the sound of the cellar door opening. He opened his eyes in time to see a body come flying toward him. He recognized the long flowing hair. "Angelina!"

He caught her, falling backward as he did. His own drowsiness was finally wearing off. The steel door slammed shut and he heard a lock slide into place before he had time to react.

He rolled with Angelina and came to rest with her on top of him. "Sweetheart, are you all right?"

She groaned. "I'm alive."

A small window, the only one to the outside world, let in enough light that he could see the black-and-blue cheek as well as other signs that she'd been worked over. "Oh, sweetheart," he whispered.

"Sweetheart?"

"Drop it, Marcus," David said.

"Marcus?" Through her haze of pain, she'd recognized that voice. Painfully Angelina rolled to her side.

"I'm here, sis."

How long had it been since she'd been called that? Tears welled in her eyes. Relief that he was alive burgeoned. Ire. Joy to see him. Bitterness.

He leaned forward from where he was sitting against one of the walls and gathered her up in his arms.

She hugged him back. She was five years old again and they'd just lost their parents. He hugged her and she clung to him. "Marcus."

"Shush. I won't let him hurt you again."

Anger at those words and old memories long-suppressed blossomed. She shoved him away. "That's a lie."

Marcus sat back stunned.

"Sweetgelina," David began and moved forward.

"No! I'm not five years old, Marcus. You can't tell me those lies and expect me to believe them."

He looked at her as if she were crazy, then said patiently, "You're still angry that I sent you back when you were sixteen."

She lunged at him, all of her pent-up fury coming out.

David intercepted her.

Pain screamed in her body, but she ignored it.

"Calm down, sweetheart."

"No! I will not calm down. How dare you say you'll protect me," she raged at Marcus. "Who needs protecting? Who needs rescuing? You do. And I won't desert you. I came here when you called, *unlike you*."

Years of anger and bitterness flowed out of her.

"I was wrong not to check up on you, but you wouldn't take my calls."

"More lies," she said scathingly. "Just like when you promised to let me come live with you when I turned eighteen. No, you didn't care. All you cared about was your Jesus. You sent me back into that hell hole with our uncle when you knew he was abusive."

Marcus paled. "He never laid a hand on you."

Angelina laughed, scornfully. "Oh? What makes you think that? You were gone. You weren't there to protect me. He had to have someone to hurt. And when I went back, he proved he could do whatever he wanted."

"No," Marcus denied it at first and then seemed to change his mind. "Why didn't you tell me?"

"You never called. You never checked up on me. At least you had an out—"

"You ran away and I couldn't find you," Marcus said getting angry himself. "And I *did* call!"

"I wouldn't stay."

"You could have waited."

Hysteria bubbled up in her. "Why? He only hit you. And you ran. Well, dear brother. When I returned home, he raped me. And you wanted me to stay. *He raped me.*"

Her dark secret came out and dead silence followed.

She jerked away from both of them and staggered over to a corner of the room where she fell down to the ground and curled up.

She hated her brother now more than ever for making her say in her anger what she'd never wanted to. She started crying.

Two strong arms came around her and she realized David had come over and lain down behind her, pulling her back against him.

She turned and clung to him—of all people.

"I'll be more than happy to kill him for you."

"He's dead. Drunk driving."

"I'll dig him up and beat him then," David said. He trembled as he stroked her back.

She shook her head and clung to him. His words meant more to her than she could tell anyone. "He's dead."

He kept rubbing her back. "Then let it go."

"But I'm—he scarred me." She shuddered.

"We all carry scars, sweetheart. They make us who we are. But Someone will take those scars for your if you'll let Him."

She shook her head, sat up and realized her brother was there as well.

Turning she faced him. "How could you send me back to him?"

His face wet with tears, he simply shook his head, mute. She'd never seen her brother cry. Not ever. How many times had her uncle slapped him or shoved him or run him down verbally. Never had she seen tears.

"I didn't know, sis. I didn't know. There were no marks." He reached out to touch her and pulled back. "Why wouldn't you take my calls?"

Her head throbbed with pain, as did her heart

and just about every part of her body—the only part that felt good was where David's arm had slipped around her waist, holding her tight, as if to protect her from the world. "You never called," she argued, a sudden horrible suspicion creeping in.

"I called every day for two weeks. He said you wouldn't come to the phone."

"He lied."

Marcus groaned, a deep, gut-wrenching sound like a wounded animal. "I thought you hated me because I wouldn't let you stay down here."

Her anger drained. "I did hate you, but because you sent me back to live with him and didn't care enough to check up on me."

Marcus reached out but again pulled back. Then, throwing caution to the wind, he grabbed Angelina and pulled her into his crushing embrace. "I'll never forgive myself," he whispered.

Angelina realized, after all these years, she was finding release from her anger. "It's not your fault. He was a manipulator and he did this." She refused to call him uncle. "Your God was always first. I just guessed that was it again."

He pulled back. "You're right that God is first in my life, sis, but I wouldn't leave you like that."

She saw Marcus wince. "What is it?"

David spoke up. "Your brother's been shot in the leg. It's pretty bad."

Marcus shifted and moved back to sit down. "Frank did it. I found out—"

"I know," Angelina said. Painfully she moved over toward the window where they had more light. She was exhausted, physically from the beating and emotionally from the scene with her brother.

"What happened upstairs?" David asked now. He reached up and touched her cheek.

"He wanted information and kept at me for it until he had to go somewhere."

"What did he want?"

Angelina shrugged. She wasn't sure how long she'd been up there—twelve hours? More? He'd come and gone, and each time he'd come, it was with more questions. "I don't think he needed all the information he tried to extract. I'd still be up there but he got a call. We interrupted his plans, weren't supposed to be here for another two days.

"That, by the way, isn't Frank. His real name, or the name I knew him by, was Hank Harrison. The name we catalog him as is Scorpion."

"Frank?" David asked.

Angelina caught David's hand, which continued to stroke her face. It hurt, though he didn't realize it did. He took that as encouragement and immediately moved to her side and slipped his arms around her. "I was so worried about you, sweetheart."

Her brother looked shocked.

She wasn't completely ready to forgive him, so she leaned back into David. He felt good and she refused to admit just how much she liked being in his arms. Somewhere along the way she'd come to think of him as her equal, not some innocent who was following her incessantly and getting in the way.

"I'm fine. I told you, I can take care of myself," she muttered.

"Of course you can," he agreed.

She nodded.

He eased up his hold, adjusting her to a more comfortable position. "Is he out to kill your president?" David asked.

"Marcus, tell me what you know," Angelina said, wanting to hear why he had called her and if that was what Scorpion was after or not.

"A few weeks ago, while I was in town, one of my informants mentioned something about

TV and how life was going to change. I realized he was trying to give me a hint without being killed. He disappeared right after that, however."

"Killed?"

Marcus shook his head. "No, he said he was moving on. He was changing his life and he asked me for the name of a preacher in Melbourne. I gave him one. Still, though, I started following the news and decided it had to be something that would interest me. He had mentioned America. The only things I could think of were the president's visit or possibly a local law about marriage where they're encouraging people to have more children."

Angelina decided not to ask why that would interest him.

"And?"

"Well, I started going back into the bars more than I'd been doing in the last couple of years. Jason approached me about a job and I sent him out to Steve. I was pretty suspicious of everything by this point. So, I kept an eye on Jason."

"My innocent brother?" Angelina scoffed.

Marcus gave her a world-weary look. "I was never innocent, sis. You just chose to ignore the fact that I had gotten into drugs and was sneaking our uncle's booze."

Shocked, Angelina studied her brother closer.

"I also tried to hide it from you."

"Well, you did a good job. I always thought of you as perfect."

He shook his head. "I was headed for juvenile hall. I hated our uncle and was even hatching plans on how to get even with him."

She gaped.

"At any rate, I kept a close eye on Jason and noted him meeting with Frank when he shouldn't have been there. I started conducting a closer investigation into Frank. It was when I found out he had been treated in Europe by a plastic surgeon that I called you."

"Why?" Angelina was confused.

"Something didn't add up. He was from Australia and had lived here several years in my area, yet no one could quite remember where he came from. Everything I could find out lined up perfectly, until a former prostitute told me about some scars he had on his face and said they were from plastic surgery. She also said not to mess with him, that he was evil."

"A former prostitute?"

He nodded. "She's a Christian now and works in the inner city in Sydney. I had to go in there for something and stopped by to see how she was doing. I just happened to mention him when we were chatting."

"Luck," she muttered.

"God," Marcus countered.

Reluctantly, she admitted, "It does sound as if Someone is on your side."

David squeezed her side and she scowled at him. She hated the smug look on his face because she'd admitted she believed in God.

"I checked out some places in Europe that she said he'd mentioned to her during, um, well… anyway, I found out he had been there. I knew you had contacts and decided to be on the safe side and call you to see if you knew about the security around the president."

"That was it?"

He nodded. "I wanted you down here to see if you recognized him. If he was an enemy, you might have papers on him and well…"

She stared. "You told me it was national security."

He shrugged. "Well it is…now."

"So you expected me to recognize him?"

He sighed, a weary sigh. "Honestly, I wasn't sure. But I had to try. I was afraid that the president was in danger and if anyone would know about him, it'd be you."

It'd be her? Yes, he would think that. And he would be right because after she'd nearly allowed the president to die years ago, she'd kept tabs on him for a while thereafter, though she'd let it lapse in recent years.

"How is your leg?" she asked, changing the subject.

"I'll live," Marcus said.

"It's badly infected," David countered.

She moved forward to see where he'd been shot. It *was* a really bad infection, and, she realized, her brother was feverish. "It needs treatment."

"Soon," David agreed.

"You were telling us about Frank," Marcus caught his sister's hand. "I'll live."

Awkwardly she looked at his hand and then at him. She forced her aching body back to where she'd been sitting, except she left a bit of room between her and David this time.

"We're in a lot of trouble. And here is why." She quickly explained about the secret government behind the governments of the world. "And Frank is only one of their hired hands. I don't know who might know about us, but if he tells anyone up the list, you can be sure we won't make it out of here alive."

"Are you sure about your facts?" David asked.

Marcus interrupted. "There have always been rumors about such things. I've heard about this group as well as others. Of course, it doesn't seem this is so fictitious now."

"What do you think quantum encryption is all about? To them it's important to control—that's how they'll maintain world domination."

She sighed. "It's like a biblical battle against evil. I was reading the Bible the other night."

"You were?" Her brother sounded surprised.

She scowled. "Don't push me, though. I have too much in my heart that I just don't think I can change."

"You don't have to change. God will do the changing for you."

She glanced to the window. "Is there any other way out?"

Marcus shook his head. "No."

She believed in God but she just wasn't sure she could let go of everything. At least not in the middle of this situation.

She forced herself to walk around the room. It

took every bit of energy. Noting the canned goods on the shelf, she asked, "Do they bring you meals?"

"You're looking at what I've survived on."

A small piece of metal to cut open the cans lay next to an opened can. Her brother looked as if he'd lost weight and had dark circles under his eyes. Evidently, they didn't care if he lived or died, which didn't bode well.

"They ever open the door?"

"Rarely and not on a schedule."

She leaned against the table and worked to catch her breath. None of her bones were broken but her face and ribs were bruised, she had a split lip and one shoulder was twisted. With the amount of pain she was in, she wouldn't be surprised if it was dislocated. "Well, I'm sure Scorpion will be back for me. He enjoys his games too much to let me go."

"You know him, don't you?" David asked and she knew what he meant.

Slowly she turned, her gaze touching on the many different things in the room. "You guessed it already. We were involved at one time when I first met him. He was only using me."

David's gaze slid away.

"Let's see, that makes me a fornicator, doesn't it?" she asked bitterly.

David stood and walked directly to stand in front of her. "I was too, as well as an alcohol-abuser. You want to compare sins?"

She simply looked at him.

He cupped her cheek. "You don't get it, sweetheart, do you? God makes us new if we ask. The sin goes into the past to be forgotten, and then He tells us to concentrate on what we do with today."

"So you care about my uncle and how I feel about him?"

Slowly he shook his head. "Only that he hurt you and I can't take that pain from you. If you haven't realized, sweetgelina, I want to protect you and I think, believe it or not, that you may need someone like me to protect you day by day."

Her eyes widened.

He grinned and leaned in for a kiss.

Marcus coughed and turned his head.

With no retort in mind, she simply looked at him coolly. "I can take care of myself."

"And how do you plan to get out of here?"

"Well, how do you expect to?" she asked.

David smiled. "Prayer."

"Prayer?" Angelina rolled her eyes.

"Why not?" Marcus asked.

"Fine. Do it." She smirked. "And then I'll work on a real way to get us out."

David nodded. "Very well." Short and simple, with no fanfare, he said, "God, we need a way out and we need You to provide a way."

Angelina simply looked at David. Slowly, she smiled. "Now that you see that that doesn't work—"

The sudden shaking of the ground nearly knocked her off her feet.

Chapter Sixteen

David staggered to his feet, waving at the plumes of dust, coughing as his gaze scanned the room. "Everyone okay?" he asked, seeing Marcus and then Angelina both still alive.

"What was that?" Angelina limped over toward the locked door and shoved on it.

"Earthquake." Marcus pushed himself weakly to his feet.

"You're kidding." She turned. "Door's still locked, but someone may come down to check on us."

David hurried over toward the door and, as if on cue, heard footsteps upstairs. He dropped to the floor near some debris.

"What—" Marcus began.

"Wait," Angelina told her brother and dropped down next to David.

The door clicked and swung open.

"We need help down here. David's been hurt."

One of the two guards came down the stairs. "Back up, girlie."

Angelina did, though David could tell her every muscle was bunched.

The guard came down, pistol in hand and, though he watched Angelina, it took only that moment when his attention turned to David for her to react. She jumped and knocked the gun from their captor's hands.

He rolled and came up right at Angelina and she ducked, avoiding his grasp.

The other guard rushed down the stairs into the fray.

David smoothly came to his feet and intercepted the second guard, snatching the gun.

He flipped the pistol. "Not so fast," he warned, as the guy started to lunge at him. He cocked it. "Back off. You too," he called to the other one who'd frozen at the sound of a gun being cocked.

Angelina ran past and scooped up the other man's gun. "Good work," she said to David and then leaned in to give him a quick kiss, surprising him. "Marcus, can you stand on your own?"

"I'm not sure for how long."

She nodded. "I'll keep them covered. David, you help get my brother upstairs."

David nodded. His heart beat fast, and his body wanted to fight. He needed to move to expend that energy. Going over, he slipped an arm around Marcus and with his eyes on the men, he carefully but quickly helped Marcus up the stairs. "Come on, Angelina," he called, finding the lock and waiting.

She backed up the stairs and both men followed. When she was out, David slammed the door and locked it. The last sight he'd seen was two angry, frustrated blokes who knew their hours were numbered to how many it took their boss to return.

"Let's get out of here." Angelina wrapped one arm around her aching ribs, the other hand still holding the pistol, and started toward the door, her eyes alert for any danger.

David kept his own pistol ready. Ignoring the pounding on the cellar door, he grabbed Marcus and together they looked for any sign of others as they left the kitchen.

Angelina paused. David moved up beside her. "What's the matter?"

"We need to look around."

David didn't question why. He knew Angelina was sharp and knew her job well. He saw another pistol on a coffee table and checked it. "Marcus, if you have to, use this."

Marcus collapsed in a chair next to a fireplace and David handed him the revolver. Through the kitchen, they could still hear the men trying to force open the cellar door. David knew how impossible that was so he wasn't worried.

Angelina checked out the downstairs room and then limped up the stairs. "Beds. Looks like no one lives here permanently."

"Men don't decorate like you sheilas." David was right behind her.

A smile cracked Angelina's face. "Whatever."

"Was that humor?"

She shook her head. "Stop distracting me."

"What are you looking for?"

"I don't know." She went into the last bedroom and paused. "But I think I just found it."

The room was filled with boxes. She opened one and pulled out wire and electronics. "They were working on something."

She saw a computer on a desk and went over to it. "Stupid people. Not even locked."

She slipped the gun in the back of her jeans and sat down, wincing as she did. David knew she was in a lot of pain, but she didn't once complain.

He was falling for the little sheila. He wasn't sure when it'd changed from a need to protect to something deeper, but it was growing there, fierce and stormy in his heart.

She typed some commands and opened up the index. In minutes, she had pulled up several articles. "What is today?"

"Thursday."

"The president arrives tomorrow."

"So it *is* him they're after?"

"Why else would they have all of this on the computer?"

She searched some more. "No e-mail capability or Internet. That would have told me a lot," she muttered.

David walked around checking out other boxes. "Papers and pens, clips—office supplies. Odd," he said. "Looks like they cleaned up the local computer store with all of these small electronic pieces."

"They were building something, but for the life of me, I can't figure out what it'd be."

Angelina turned from the computer. "I doubt Scorpion is going to be back before tomorrow. I imagine he's on his way to Sydney to hole up for the president."

"What's our plan?"

"To get to Sydney and try to stop him."

"Why not call your boss?"

"Former boss. He won't listen, but believe me, when we get to Sydney, I plan to do just that."

She started to leave. David caught her arm. "I want to tell you something, sweetheart, before we go back downstairs."

She paused, eyebrow raised. "Yes?"

His heart beat so hard he was afraid it was going to come right out of his chest. In frustration, he pulled her forward and kissed her.

She blinked, then her eyes fluttered shut and she accepted the kiss.

When he pulled back, he stared at how soft and gentle she looked, her eyes half-closed, lips soft and not hardened from the worries of the world. He leaned back down and kissed the injured lip ever so gently.

She blinked.

She blinked again. "You don't think you could have chosen a more appropriate time to kiss me?"

He sighed in frustration. "With you? When is there ever an appropriate time? It doesn't matter anyhow. We'd better go."

He closed off all emotions and shoved his feelings away. He knew where this emotional tide was taking him. "You're right. We need to concentrate on now."

He headed toward the hallway and Angelina watched him go. She didn't know what to say. His tenderness spoke volumes. Did she love him? Yes. Maybe. Did she even understand love? She knew in the past few days with David she'd felt a type of peace she didn't quite understand. She watched him and in a way was jealous of how easygoing he was and how things simply rolled off his shoulders.

She took a deep breath and started after David, but he was already downstairs. "We're about ready here," he said and helped Marcus to his feet.

His declaration was as if the moment upstairs had never happened, she thought, except for one tiny flash in his eyes as he glanced at her.

Man, she thought, her entire world turning upside down. This stranger had become her friend and her equal, a protector when she needed it. How had it all happened so fast?

When had it happened?

She was suddenly seeing David in an entirely new light. He was more than someone along with her. He was a very handsome man.

She really didn't need this right now, she thought, disgruntled.

"The pounding has stopped," she noted. "I guess they realize they're going to be down there for a while."

She went to the front door and looked out. A small sporty coupe sat there, contrasting to the desolate rural area around them.

David opened the door and together he and Marcus went down the stairs to the overgrown lawn in front.

"Where are we?" Angelina asked, heading to the car.

"Not sure," David said and helped Marcus into the back seat where he could prop his leg up.

Surprising her, Marcus answered. "We're over a day away from Sydney."

"How do you know that?"

"I was awake when they brought me out here.

The nearest town is about six hours, if I remember correctly. Then Sydney will be about another twelve hours past that. And it's almost 8:00 p.m."

"That late?" Angelina slipped under the dash and pulled some wires. "Don't suppose anyone saw car keys, did they?"

"Probably in the bloke's pocket."

She nodded.

David hurried back into the house and came back out with a knife.

"I was just going to go looking for that," Angelina said awkwardly.

He still acted as if nothing had passed between them only a short time before. "No keys, but I figured you could use this."

"Thanks." She relaxed a bit and concentrated on the wires. In only a couple of minutes, she had the engine going.

David tapped her shoulder. "Better let me drive since you aren't used to our roads."

She nodded and slipped out of the driver's side. Going around she slid into the comfortable seat. "This is much better than shifting."

David put the car into Reverse and turned the wheel. "I didn't look for any pain meds, sweetheart. Can you make it to the next town?"

She nodded. "Marcus?"

"After living down there in that cellar for who knows how long, believe me, I can make it."

She glanced at David, not so sure. Marcus's voice was weak and thready. And he hadn't been able to walk on his own. He was much worse off than he let on. And he was hotter than he had been earlier. His temperature was going up.

David nodded. "We'll make it," he said softly. "Don't you worry, sweetgelina. We haven't come this far to fail."

Angelina hoped that was the case. Her brother's life and the president's hung in the balance, and her future was now hanging before her.

She didn't see how all three could have a happy ending.

But at least things were finally going their way.

Chapter Seventeen

"There is no way we could have run out of gas." Angelina paced away from the vehicle into the dark chilly night. Both hands on her hips, she stared up at the starry night.

The sound of crunching underbrush echoed in the night air and then stopped as David stood beside her. His gaze went to the stars as well. "They must have had gas back at the house somewhere."

"Or that's where Scorpion went, not to Sydney but to run an errand and get gas, which would mean he already knows we're gone."

"At least we didn't take the main road."

"Yeah but then no one will find us out here either."

David stood so close and yet it felt as if there

was a gulf between them. She'd never been so unsure of anything in her life. Her in-charge attitude had suddenly deserted her leaving her uncertain how to act around him.

It frustrated her—especially when she had so many other things she needed to be concentrating on.

"You're worried about Marcus?"

Angelina glanced toward David. He no longer studied the stars but studied her. She sighed. Glancing back toward the car, she lowered her voice. "I don't know if he's going to make it."

David's mouth turned down, his face grim. "We've got to trust God, sweetheart."

"That's just it, I never have. How can I trust a God who took my brother away?"

She could tell David didn't have an answer.

"How far is the town?"

He glanced back out in the distance. "Maybe half the night, if Marcus can make it."

Angelina glanced back at her brother.

"Go talk to him, sweetheart. He can help you work out what we need to do."

She glanced at David. He had a look in his eyes she didn't understand, but she nodded. Still, she hesitated.

He grinned. "I think I'll go take care of nature's call while you talk."

She rolled her eyes. Typical David. Easygoing attitude and knew how to make her smile.

She walked back over to the car. Marcus had managed to shift to lie in the back seat, propped up against one door so he could see what was going on.

She shoved the front seat forward and crawled in to check his leg. "How's it feeling?"

Marcus shifted to make room for his sister. "Like it's on fire," he replied.

Reaching for his leg, she moved aside the torn piece of cloth to examine the wound more closely. From the starlight, she could see it was swollen and red. It still surprised her not to see a boy's but a man's leg lying there.

"What are you thinking?"

Angelina glanced up at her brother. The young innocence of childhood was gone, replaced by the mature look of someone who had lived many years. "Just that you've grown up since I last saw you."

Marcus chuckled. "Imagine how I feel. My little awkward sister is now a beautiful take-charge woman."

"Yes, but then you kept tabs on me, didn't you, so you had an idea of what I looked like."

His smile faded. "I wish I could change the past."

Aching, she reached forward to cover the spot on his leg. She was that little sister again, needing her big brother. Marcus realized that, caught her hand and pulled her forward. She hugged him back, embarrassed, yet wanting to feel that older-brother hug.

"I can't, Angie. I wish I could, but there's no way to go back. If you'd let go of the pain though—"

"How? How do I do that?"

He stroked her back, running his hand down her hair over and over. "Our uncle was an evil man. Hate and bitterness consumed him. I don't know why he wanted to make everyone around him miserable, except that he was miserable himself. You know the saying. Misery—"

"—loves company." She laughed bitterly. "He did his best to make sure we were miserable."

"Then why let him?"

"What?"

She started to pull back, but he tightened his hold. "Listen, sis. Just listen."

He stroked her hair again and she found herself relaxing, just as she'd done when she was five, six, and seven and he'd do the same thing when she was scared.

"Your bitterness and anger. It's giving him victory every time you're angry at him, every time you pull away from a man or a relationship, every time you blame God, it's saying that our uncle won the fight."

"No way!" She pulled, but he didn't let go.

"Yes. Because you're doing the same thing he did. You're being miserable, conforming to what he wanted."

"That's not true." This time he did release her when she pulled back.

"Oh? Then he didn't say repeatedly that God didn't care? That he could do whatever he wanted, and God wouldn't stop him? He didn't tell us that we were worthless and would never amount to anything? That no one would ever have you?"

"Stop it!" All of her uncle's old insults came pounding back at her. "I don't have to hear that anymore. I left, remember?"

He nodded. "You left, but you took him with you—in your heart. He's affected every choice you've made. You need to let go of that."

"You don't think I've tried?" Angry, she felt tears coming. "You don't think there isn't a day that I get up and say 'Today he's not going to affect me'?"

Slowly, Marcus nodded. "But you can't let go, can you?"

"So why are you doing this?" Angelina demanded. She had only wanted comfort from her brother, instead it seemed he was determined to torment her.

"If you'll simply ask God, He'll help you let go of the pain and forgive our uncle."

"Forgive? He doesn't deserve my forgiveness!"

"Not for him, Angelina, but for you. You forgive him so you won't hurt anymore. But only God can help you."

She shook her head. "I can't do it."

"Then you let our uncle rule your life?"

"He does not!"

"Then tell me why you can't accept that you're falling for David?"

Like an arrow hitting its target, Marcus's words pierced her heart.

She pulled back.

Marcus reached for her.

She managed to avoid his grasp and climb out

of the car. Before he heard the sob, she turned and headed off into the brush.

David was just walking up. "Angelina?"

She didn't answer. He started to follow.

"Let her go."

David hesitated and then turned to Marcus and demanded, "What did you say to her?"

"Only the truth."

"You—"

"Only led her to God."

David's shoulders collapsed, the anger easing a bit. He looked back to where Angelina had disappeared into the night. "You didn't have to make her cry." David felt helpless, torn between going after her to fix things and smacking Marcus for making her cry.

"If it'd make you feel better to belt me, go ahead," Marcus said wryly.

The last of David's anger drained away. "She's hurting, Marcus."

"Believe me, David, I know that better than anyone. But the only way that hurt is going to subside is through God."

"And making her cry was the way to do it?" He still wasn't ready to forgive Marcus for making Angelina weep.

"She had to come to a point where she realized she was still carrying our uncle around in her. I heard her say something about her scars more than once to you. She needs to accept that she hasn't let go of the past."

David agreed, but he didn't like the way Marcus had gone about it. "I leave you for one minute and come back to find her sobbing." He shook his head.

"But I think she's finally ready to talk to God and let go."

David looked at Marcus, hopeful. "You really think so?"

Marcus nodded.

David noticed how pale and weak Marcus looked in the moonlight. "Are you going to be able to make it to the next town?"

Marcus opened his eyes and gave David a gentle smile. "'My God shall supply all my needs according to His riches in glory.'"

"And just what do you mean by that?" Consternation flashed on David's face.

"You know exactly what I mean."

"Are you going to tell Angelina?"

"I think she already knows."

David shook his head. "She's not going to leave you behind."

"There's always hope, David. Make her understand that. You need to worry about the president now. Because of this setback, it'll be amazing if she makes it to Sydney in time."

"What are you talking about?"

David turned and saw Angelina standing there, her face tear-stained, but glowing as if she'd found release.

"You've let go?" he asked going forward.

Surprised, both eyebrows shot up. "How can you—never mind." She shook her head. "I want to know what you meant about me making it to Sydney."

David glanced at Marcus. He felt like a coward, not wanting to tell Angelina. But, as weak as Marcus was, he couldn't let Marcus explain either. "Marcus can't make the trip."

There, he'd said it.

Angelina simply stared at him. "Of course he can't. We'll have to leave him at the next town."

"You don't understand, sis," Marcus said from inside the car. "I can't make that trip either."

A heartbeat of silence followed. Then Angelina piped up. "I don't understand."

"I can't go to the next town. I'm not strong enough."

"That's why we'll help you," Angelina argued.

Marcus stared deeply into his sister's eyes. "You can't help me to the next town, sis. I won't be able to make the trip."

She shook her head. "Of course you will."

"No, Angie, I won't."

She paused again, and David saw the flash of desperation in her eyes. "But I just found you again, Marcus. You don't have a choice."

Marcus held out his hand.

Angelina hesitated, and then, before David's eyes, turned into a scared younger sister. She climbed into the back seat and crawled into her brother's arms. "I won't leave you, Marcus."

"Shhh, sis," Marcus said gently and ran his hands down her back. "You know that you've been trained all of your life to be strong and protect the president. Inadvertently our uncle taught us both how to be tough. In his attempt to destroy us, we learned strength. And you have to call on that strength now. God will buoy it and take care of you and make sure you get to where you're going."

"I can't leave you, Marcus." Her voice cracked with emotion.

"You have to, sis."

She cried and hugged her brother tight.

"'I know whom I have believed in and am persuaded that he is able to keep me...against this world.'"

"What's that?" she asked and David heard the tears in her voice.

"A song I learned. He'll keep me, sis and He'll keep you."

"But—"

"I'm ready. I've run the race, as the saying goes. Paul tells us that to live in Christ and to die is gain. Honey, it's great to live, but just think about how wonderful it'll be to be in God's arms. It is indeed something to gain. No more pain, no more sorrow. And to know that you'll now be there with me one day—"

She cried.

David swallowed, his throat tight with emotion.

Marcus held his sister for the longest time before finally pushing her away. "Go, sis. You have to go now or you're not going to have time to save our president."

She shook her head, tears running down her face.

Marcus looked past her to David.

David did the hardest thing he'd done in his life. He stepped forward and pulled Angelina from Marcus. "We have to go."

"I can't!"

David wrapped his arms around Angelina. Whispering into her hair, he said, "Let the last image your brother sees be of strength."

She shuddered. "Marcus…"

David squeezed her. Over her head, he could see Marcus had tears on his face.

She shuddered again and swallowed. He heard it. And she took in several breaths before the shudders passed.

Looking up into David's eyes, she acknowledged that he could let her go, that she was under control.

He nodded and released her.

She turned and faced Marcus. "I want to say so many things…"

"I know," Marcus said when she didn't continue. His voice was weak and his breathing labored.

"I guess what I have to say is that I love you, Marcus, and I never stopped loving you, no matter how angry I was."

"I know." He smiled weakly, one arm lying limply across his abdomen.

She smiled, though David could feel every muscle in her body tense. "And I have to say thank you for showing me the Way. I wish I could tell you everything I went through a short time ago as I faced God for the first time—"

"I'll find out soon enough."

She shuddered, then forced a laugh. "Just make sure God tells you what I said about you."

Marcus's gaze turned soft. "I will." His eyes fluttered closed.

"I love you. I'm going to send someone back for you. I won't believe you're not waiting."

"You do that," Marcus said, but David could tell Marcus didn't believe he would be alive when they found him.

"You said it yourself," Angelina argued. "God can keep you, and I'm going to ask God to keep you safe until someone arrives."

"Sweetheart, we need to go." David was dying inside watching the interaction, and though he wanted to give Angelina more time, he also wanted to spare her the agony as well.

"I know," she said to David.

Turning back one last time to Marcus, she said, "Promise me, you'll try to hold on."

"Angie—"

"Promise me! Or I won't move from here."

Marcus held his tongue. Finally, he sighed. "I promise."

She nodded. Then with one last determined look, she said, "I will see you again."

Turning, she headed off into the night. David gave one last look to his best friend, wishing he'd had time to tell Marcus just how much he meant to him.

"Take care of my sister," Marcus said.

David nodded. "I will."

He then turned and headed out after Angelina, part of his heart staying behind with the man who had led him to the Lord, the man who had changed his life.

Chapter Eighteen

"It's got to be close to four in the morning."

"Almost five," David agreed. He pointed to the stars.

She paused to look up at the sky. "Nothing is familiar to me."

"I just can't imagine that," David murmured.

Angelina took a deep breath, slapping her hands around her to ward off the cold, and started walking again. "How much further?"

"Since we weren't on the main way, I'm not quite sure, but I'm guessing we're within half an hour of the town."

"I haven't seen any traffic."

"We should be coming to the road soon."

They trudged onward for a short time before David asked, "How much pain are you in?"

She grimaced. "I've been in worse."

"We could stop for a break," he offered.

She shook her head. "I need to get to the town to send back help for my brother."

David sighed. "You know he's probably—"

"Don't say it."

"You'll have to face it sooner or later, sweetheart."

She stopped and turned on him. "Later would be fine with me."

He stopped in his tracks to avoid running into her. Letting out a weary breath he reached out to her. She went willingly into his arms. Funny, she thought, how easily she'd gotten used to doing that. "We'll be there soon and I'll personally see that someone is sent out immediately."

"I'm sorry," Angelina murmured into his warm chest.

"No need to apologize, sweetheart. I should be the one offering those words. I remember losing my parents, and though I never had a brother, if I did, it would be Marcus."

"Then how can you so easily dismiss him?" Angelina asked.

"I'm not dismissing him. I just don't want you to get your hopes up and then…" He hesitated and then said more softly, "You've had that too much in your life. And I promised your brother I'd help you get to the president."

She hugged him tighter. "You're warm."

"And you, sweetgelina, are chilled."

"I still can't adjust to how chilly it is here."

She released him and started walking again.

Before David could comment, bright lights appeared in the distance. "I think we've found the road—and a car. Hurry up."

Angelina didn't argue but stepped up the pace as well. David passed her to lead the way. However, just as they approached the road, she pulled David back. "Wait."

He turned at the pull on his arm to look at her. "What?"

"How big is this town we're approaching?" Her gaze slipped off down the road as if she could see it.

"I'm not sure but probably a few hundred people." His gaze followed hers.

"Would most people be up this early?"

David thought about it and then pulled his pistol. Angelina did the same.

They hunkered down out of sight and waited. "It could be a farmer." David considered the possibility and discarded it.

"Or it could be someone delivering something to your local store here?" Angelina asked, deciding with him that it wasn't a farmer.

David shook his head. "Not likely. Wrong type of vehicle."

The moon had set and the first hint of the approaching dawn showed in the distance.

Angelina and David got their first look at the car as it began to move toward them. David voiced what he was certain Angelina feared. "Frank?"

Angelina shook her head. "No. But I do think the car is familiar…"

"Jason!" He recognized the car as one from the mission.

"His car, but it can't be him. He's dead," Angelina said tersely. "Duck."

David did and they watched as the car came within range. Two shadowy figures were inside. David knew immediately who they had to be. "How'd they escape?"

"I don't know," Angelina said and when the car was past, she eased back up. "My question is, did they find my brother and if so, do they realize we're headed this way?"

"They've probably called Frank."

"If they could get a line out, but that isn't likely. Phone lines were cut."

David didn't ask who had cut the phone lines or how she knew this. He hoped she was right and not just guessing. "I'll guarantee you there's not good cell reception out there, too. So do you think we have a chance to get to the town and maybe even Sydney before they inform him we've escaped?"

"Doubtful, since we're on foot, unless they're determined to find us without alerting Scorpion."

"I doubt *I'd* tell him that I lost us." David glanced sideways at her. "It seems his boys don't get a second chance when they mess up."

Angelina nodded. "Perceptive of you. Shall we go?"

David stood and reached down for Angelina's hand. Gently he helped her up.

She grimaced in pain as she stood. "At least we have a road to follow."

"It'll make the walking easier on you."

"Yes." She confirmed his suspicion. Going across the rough terrain as they had only increased her pain. She'd been limping more and he'd noticed her arm gripping her ribs a bit more forcefully the last few miles. And her steely gaze was now more a grimace.

He slipped an arm around her. She started to protest but he shook his head. "We're not too far now. Look up ahead."

In the growing dawn, the outline of a house was visible. And beyond that, several small buildings dotted the area. "The town?"

"Oh, it's bigger than that, sweetheart. But that is the outlying area."

He felt her relax against him. "Finally."

As they hurried up the road, David admitted he'd blown it earlier yesterday by giving in to that kiss. He'd jumped the gun, since she hadn't sorted out her feelings for God.

She'd been so awkward and not sure how to act around him. But now, as they'd traveled the desert, her pain had pushed through her fear and she was leaning on him once again. And he was glad that she'd forgotten her awkwardness and was once again allowing him to touch her.

He wanted to protect her and love her, but his declaration would put them into danger. Now was not the time.

"A light just came on in that house."

David looked ahead to where she pointed. "Looks like someone is starting to rise for the morning."

"They'll have a phone."

"Yeah."

"I hope they don't mind early-morning guests." Angelina broke free and with determined strides headed toward the house that was her beacon of hope.

"Er—" David started, then shrugged. Maybe they wouldn't shoot her for pounding on their door this early in the morning. He hurried to catch up to her just as she entered the small fence that surrounded the yard.

Angelina climbed the steps and knocked.

"Let me do—" David started.

The door opened a crack and then wider. "Oh, my! What have you done to yourself? Look at you!"

The woman, her hair in curlers and wearing a cotton gown, threw open the door and reached for Angelina. "Daddy, we have company," she called out.

"Thank you," Angelina said to the woman. Noticing her accent, she added, "You're not Australian."

"And you aren't either. However, we consider ourselves Australian now. We've lived here nearly twenty years. I'm Georgia."

"Angelina."

"David," David said.

"Now you *are* from here," Georgia said and smiled.

An older man, in jeans and a flannel shirt, appeared in the hallway. "Mornin'," he said.

"I need to use your phone. My brother is stuck out in the wilderness several miles from here. He needs—" her voice caught. "He needs help."

"Oh, honey," Georgia said. "Come on in here. This here David can give directions to my husband."

She slipped her arm around Angelina and clucking over her like a mother hen, guided her into the other room.

David turned to the man. "David Lemming."

He held out his hand and the man shook it. "Call me Hooter. Everyone around here does. We're originally from Hooters, Alabama, and folks thought that amusing."

How odd, David thought. "Hooter," he acknowledged.

"So what happened to you folks? Car accident?"

David sighed and ran a hand through his short sandy hair. "Would you believe we ran out of gas?" His features darkened. "Marcus was too weak to travel. I'm afraid he is probably…" His voice trailed off.

The other man sobered. "I'll get my hat and shoes."

David stopped him. "I need to ask you a big favor."

Hooter paused, his wizened gaze studying David. David glanced past him to where the women had disappeared. "I know this is going to sound crazy, but the American president's life is in danger."

Hooter's bushy eyebrows rose. "You say?"

David winced, not sure what he meant. "I could take time to explain the entire situation, but suffice it to say that Angelina Harding used to work for the Secret Service. Her brother, a local missionary here, had information. She came here but the terrorist had already taken her brother. We only found him when they captured us. Now we're trying to get to Sydney and we have no transportation and her brother is probably dead several kilometers back."

"You're right there, David. That does sound

like a whopper. But seeing the black-and-blue on the woman adds credibility to your story, and I believe you. You give me directions and I'll go for her brother—dead or alive he doesn't deserve to be left out there, God rest his soul. In the meantime, you clean up, and then you can borrow our second vehicle."

Shocked, David stared. "To take to Sydney?"

Hooter nodded. "Our president is in danger. We're American citizens, remember?" he said, and David had actually forgotten. "And I imagine Secret Service is the best to handle this, so you take that woman on up there to see her boss."

"Thank you."

"David," Angelina appeared.

David nodded to Hooter who turned and shuffled back down the hall to finish dressing. When he was gone, David turned back to Angelina.

She came forward. "He's going to go retrieve your brother."

Relief wilted her, but only for a moment. He could see that she was torn as she said next, "I called Washington and my former boss is out. I talked to other agents and they said they'd get the message to him. I don't think they'll take it seriously though. Even if they do, we need to get to

Sydney. They aren't going to recognize Scorpion after his surgery."

David agreed. "Hooter said we could borrow his truck—"

She shook her head. "I have a better idea."

"Oh?"

"Georgia knows a man who is a crop duster—"

"Flying?"

Angelina paused. "You're not scared of flying, are you?"

He grinned. "I'm sure not, sweetheart." He reached out and hugged her.

She blinked.

"Have I mentioned just how resourceful you are?"

She smiled slyly. "I *was* in the Secret Service."

David chuckled.

"Georgia is fixing a very quick breakfast. She insists on feeding us—I think she's *plum tickled* to see an American and wants to practice her Southern hospitality."

"You Americans," David said fondly.

"You Aussies," she replied and cupped his cheek.

His eyes darkened. "You don't want to start something now," he warned and leaned down to kiss her.

"Yes, I do," she argued and leaned in to kiss him.

The kiss was tender and filled with emotion that he realized Angelina wasn't able to express yet. She would, in time, he thought as he pulled back.

"Now, if you don't mind, I'm going to shower. Georgia said she has some clothes of her daughter's that just might fit me. And we can eat while we're waiting for the plane."

David simply shook his head. She turned and he followed her to the kitchen where Georgia was waiting.

Chapter Nineteen

"This way." Angelina tugged on David's hand as they wove their way through the crowded streets of Sydney. They'd gone as far as they could by cab and now were walking the rest of the way.

"Security is certainly tight."

Angelina nodded. "After 9/11 things changed. I hope the increase in security is also because of my call."

"At least you were able to cover the bruises," he commented, "or we might not have made it this far."

Angelina paused to look back at him. "We still may not with the way you're dressed."

He growled.

She chuckled. "Although, dress pants, a jacket and a shirt that are a bit too short and just a tad tight might come into vogue eventually."

"She did offer to wash my clothes."

"We didn't have time to wait," Angelina said in amusement. Turning the corner, they finally arrived at the city center where the president would be. Angelina had seen Air Force One at the airport so she knew he'd already landed. She'd even gone over to get a message to someone, but they wouldn't let her near the tarmac. In frustration, she'd given up, realizing she was wasting precious time.

Here in Sydney, the president was supposed to be meeting with a group of international businessmen, according to the paper, then several private appointments before meeting with the prime minister of Australia. A few things were on the agreed agenda: among them encryption technology. The president had only partial support in Australia and he hoped to gain some of the business sector's backing, not only in Australia but also other countries around the world.

"Earth calling," David whispered.

Angelina glanced sideways at him. "I'm sorry. I was just thinking over the president's itinerary that I was able to pull from the paper. I'm sure there are Secret Service agents out here somewhere. I just need to spot one."

"Are they that easy to spot?" David asked, surprised.

"For someone who's been in the business, yes."

He nodded.

"Ms. Harding?"

"Unless they spot us first," she said to David and turned. "I need to talk to Jennings."

The man was tall and blended in well. She knew David wouldn't have noticed him unless he'd noticed the earpiece. The man spoke into his collar. "We're bringing her in."

"He's with me," Angelina said and grabbed David.

The man didn't respond. Angelina started along beside him, David going with her.

"Where are we going?" David asked in a low voice as they walked together.

"I hope to see my former boss, Jennings."

"You think he'll listen?"

Angelina nodded. "I think he will. Otherwise he wouldn't be bringing us in—"

"That's reassuring."

"Jennings may be stubborn," she offered, "but he's not stupid. If he really perceives this as a threat, he'll listen."

"Good to know."

They passed through the crowds and with a flash of an ID, slipped into a building.

The building was air-conditioned despite the cool weather outside, and the halls were lined with all kinds of security. She knew the drill well. They passed a media room where many news people mingled, drinking coffee, smoking, chatting, trying to find out who knew what. None noticed them as they walked by, she realized thankfully. Servers, housecleaning—the halls were full of all kinds of threats, and each one had been meticulously scrutinized before ever showing up for work.

The chandeliers glowed and the rich draperies were pulled back, allowing in the southern sun that shone brightly. Rich carpet muffled their steps and mahogany tables, waxed to a shine, reflected their silhouettes as they passed.

They stopped in a small room and were scanned head to toe with electronics.

"They're clean."

Their leader nodded and then motioned for them to continue out the door and down the hall.

At the elevator the man they were with, along with another one they'd picked up, both flashed IDs. Once in the elevator, one pushed the button for the eleventh floor.

David glanced curiously at Angelina, waiting for her to say something, but she wasn't saying a word. She knew enough to be careful of what she said, since she didn't know these people.

When the bell dinged and the door opened, two security guards stood there waiting. "It's okay," she said to David in reassurance and together they stepped out.

They followed the men down the hall, the other two behind them. David glanced behind him wondering at so many escorts but decided this must be normal given the circumstances.

He hoped.

A door near the middle of the corridor had two guards in front of it and David grinned, thinking "Two by two they entered the ark," wondering if the door was their ark.

Sure enough, the two in front of them paused and one reached out, nodded and opened the door.

"Thanks, Stravinsky," Angelina said, mockingly.

One man cracked a slight grin before returning to his position at the door.

As they entered, the two men behind them turned and left. There were still a good dozen agents in the room, moving around, monitoring equipment, and talking into mikes.

One of the two in front motioned. "In the side room over there."

Angelina boldly walked forward, purely professional, and David followed. He was way out of his league.

Someone else opened a door, and they passed into a quiet room where only two people sat chatting.

Charts and reports sat on a desk, there were four rich comfortable chairs, two sofas, a coffee machine, ice and a separate bathroom. Silk trees and a silk rubber plant were artfully displayed. The closed curtains kept out the sun.

The first man was a younger man, short military blond hair, dressed in black dress pants and a shirt with a stiff stand-up collar. He wore nice cuff links and looked to be around thirty years old. The second man was thin, balding, with an angular face. He wore gray pants and a white shirt, cuff links as well. His gray loafers had tassels and David believed they were the brand he used to buy. He also thought it was a safe assumption that he was the boss, the way he quickly assessed him before turning his gaze to Angelina.

"Hello, Jennings."

He would have been right. The man leaned back in his chair. "Been a long time, Harding."

"You were expecting us."

He glanced briefly at David then back at her. "I was expecting you. What made you bring him in?"

"I needed an insider who could get me around, and he fit the bill."

David bristled.

"He's safe."

"We know that," the other man said.

"I'm David Lemming," he said into the room, a bit put off with the way they spoke as if he weren't there.

"We know that too," the man said.

"You haven't changed a bit, Walters," Angelina said coolly to the other man, and then crossed to one of the chairs and sat down. She wasn't relaxing, however, she was stiff and alert, reading to pounce at the least provocation. "What's going on?"

David quietly moved to seat himself near her,

not liking the two men despite the fact they were supposed to be the good guys. He moved in close to Angelina and waited.

Jennings glanced once more at David and then focused on Angelina. "We've been watching for Scorpion. If, as you said, he's here, then we know he'll work hard to get revenge. However, we haven't seen anything."

"He's changed his appearance."

The two men exchanged glances. "We figured as much."

"We've also found out more. He's only a small man on a much bigger scale."

Jennings glanced at Walters then back to Angelina.

"What are you talking about?" Walters asked.

Jennings leaned back in his chair. "Want some coffee?"

Angelina stared hard at Jennings. "I don't drink coffee, but David likes tea."

Alert, because he knew that was a lie; Angelina did drink coffee, David nodded. "It is cold out, and I do think I'd like a spot of hot tea with milk and sugar."

Jennings frowned. "Walters, get us some tea please."

He started to object then held his tongue and stood. "Be right back."

Jennings waited until Walters left. "So what is it you think you know?"

"Ever heard of the tribunary commission?"

Jennings stared at Angelina for so long David thought he wasn't going to answer. Just as he opened his mouth to comment, Jennings said, "No, and neither have you, or anyone else in this room. Is that clear?"

He'd surprised Angelina. "But—"

The door opened up. "Stravinsky is getting tea."

Walters came over and seated himself. "So what were you talking about?"

Jennings glanced at him. "The meetings the president has scheduled. Angelina is certain that Scorpion is being paid to take him out again."

David wondered what had just happened and studied Walters. Did Jennings not trust his own men?

"What makes you think that?" Walters asked sharply.

Angelina shrugged. "As I said earlier, Scorpion had surgery, changed his name and has been hiding here for years. Ever heard of—"

"We've checked everyone out that you've come in contact with—or we're trying to at this point," Walters cut in. "What we need to know is what he looks like."

Angelina cast a scathing look at Walters. "Sorry, but I didn't think to take a picture. I was too busy trying to save my brother." Her gaze darkened.

Jennings had the grace to look apologetic as he said, "Wish we could have saved him. We heard he was left behind."

David wasn't going to ask how they knew, though the question burned in him.

"We can get a sketch artist up here and get you to give us a description—"

"Let us find him." David had kept quiet as long as possible and decided to state the obvious.

All eyes turned to David.

"Just how do you expect to do that?" Jennings asked.

David looked at the men and then shook his head. "I used to travel in these circles. I have a lot of money—which I'm sure you know. Many of these businessmen I've probably met in my years as a rancher. You know, ranchers do use computers to track their animals. Chips in them and such."

The two men glanced at each other.

"That's not a good idea."

Surprised, David looked at the objector. "And why not, sweetheart?"

She scowled.

Jennings gaped and Walters covered a cough. Angelina scowled at the two men. Evidently, they knew well her rules about calling her by endearments. His chest swelled a little more that he'd gotten away with it.

"You're not trained for such situations," she retorted.

"Oh? And just who helped save your cute little—"

"Don't say it," Angelina warned.

"—smiling face," he continued with a slight smile, "when we were trapped in that cellar?"

She stood. "It's ridiculous. He's not trained and I wouldn't put him in danger. You know what he'd do if he thought David was involved. It's astonishing that Scorpion let him live when he was questioning me."

David leaned back in his chair, curious as to why she objected so strenuously.

"I think you may have an idea there," Jennings said to David with a curious glance toward Angelina. "Your records do indicate you are well-known in Sydney and with several of the businessmen who are here. And Angelina is still familiar enough with our list of suspects and world leaders that she could probably identify the rest. And two sets of eyes down there are better than thirty who've never seen the new Scorpion."

"What?" Angelina turned and paced the room. "You won't give me a moment of your time on the phone, but the minute we show up, you're willing to send me and someone with no experience into the field. Why?" She whirled. "Unless you're using us as bait. That's it, isn't it?" She stared directly at Jennings. "We're bait."

"The president's life might be in jeopardy." Jennings didn't deny her charge.

"And so you're going to put David's life in jeopardy too?"

"It's my choice, isn't it?" David asked.

"No!" she said.

"Yes," the two men agreed.

"And it'd be your life in danger as well," David added quietly.

Angelina turned to say something, then threw up her hands.

David realized with blinding clarity what her problem was. Before he could comment, she turned to Jennings, indicating their outfits. "He can't go like that, and I can't go in this."

He smiled. "We can take care of that, but we need to hurry. Our friend will be arriving within the hour."

And that was that.

They were going in and Angelina didn't have a thing to say.

Or so David thought.

Chapter Twenty

"I still don't agree with you being here," Angelina muttered into the mike she wore on her formal gown. She circulated, a glass of water in her hand as she scanned the crowd for a familiar and deadly face. Her hair had been quickly styled to match the elegance of her no-nonsense long black sheath, cut up the side so she could move more easily.

David was gorgeous in a black suit and white shirt that looked as if it'd been tailored for him. She hated him at the moment—actually, it wasn't hate but absolute fear that something was going to happen to him. Scorpion would torture him if he figured out just how much David had come to mean to her. He'd made her life miserable with his mind games when they'd been together.

"Relax, sweetheart," she heard in her tiny hidden earpiece. "I'm used to this."

"You might be used to mingling, but I don't like you in harm's way."

"Why is that?" David asked lightly, and she wasn't sure whether he was speaking to her or to someone who now stood near him.

"Enough chattering," crackled in her ears. "Just watch for Scorpion, *sweetheart*."

"Funny, Stravinsky," she muttered and smiled at someone who passed.

She hated this. Hated it, hated it, hated it! Nothing here had bothered her until this.

And David asked her why.

Why did it bother her?

That was easy.

Scorpion had tried to take her heart and turn it inside out. She'd been so full of anger at her uncle that she'd been an easy target for Hank, as he called himself then. He'd showered her with love and affection, but had fed her anger at her brother—she could see that now. Then he'd convinced her that many of the men she worked with were chauvinist pigs. He'd easily swayed her to those views, and she'd naively allowed it. He was another reason she was so hard. And then when she'd seen him standing there, about to shoot the then vice president, she'd been so shocked and devastated she hadn't been able to react.

"He'll come after you because of how I feel," she muttered aloud, not even realizing she'd said it out loud.

"How do you feel?"

She heard those words from behind her and turned to see an old acquaintance standing there. She pasted a false smile on her face and said, "I feel—" and stopped.

The president was now directly in her view and sitting at a table not fifteen feet from her. Secret Service agents were near, as were businessmen. Someone had asked for an autograph—it was always happening.

She saw a hand reach for a pocket and recognized that hand. It was the ring, the ring that had cut her under the eye.

Her gaze shot up through the people around the president. "It's him."

"Pardon me?" the person near her said.

She pushed past him. "He's there. By the president," she called into the mike.

In her peripheral vision she saw David coming across the room. Secret Service agents' hands went to their ears as they heard the conversation barked over their earpieces.

In slow motion, she saw the confusion among them.

"Who? Who!"

"Where?"

"Him?"

Questions overlapped.

The men around the president started looking around.

"A pen!" It coalesced in her mind what she'd seen at the house. "Stop him from getting his pen out. That's how he's going to get the president. The ring. See the ring," and she shot off a description. "Behind Jackson." She recognized that ring. It was very distinctive. And they would easily recognize it, if they could see it.

She ran now, shoving at people.

Scorpion knew suddenly. He knew.

His gaze shot up and met hers.

He flashed fury and then smiled as his hand came out of his jacket, pen in hand. "Stop him!" she cried out loud.

Confusion erupted.

People screamed as they sensed something going on.

The pen pointed toward the president even as she leapt over the table. Other Secret Service agents lunged for Scorpion as she lunged for the president.

She hit the Commander-in-Chief in a body slam, knocking him to the ground. Someone flew over her.

"It's okay," she shouted at the president. "Get him out of here!" she called out and felt others grabbing at the arms of the president and dragging him from under her and away, and as they did, she realized this time—not like the last time—this time *she* had saved his life.

And she saw the acknowledgment in his eyes, just before he disappeared in a swarm of suits.

She leapt back up to her feet and turned, just in time to see Scorpion hitting the ground.

"Thank heavens!" someone cried out near her.

"Is he dead? Is he safe!" another shouted.

Angelina could pick out David from among the confused crowd. She rushed to his side, her gaze on Scorpion.

He looked up at her and grinned even as Jackson cuffed him. "They got him," she said to David. "He didn't hurt the president."

She turned to David and saw his face, ashen with pain.

"But he got me, sweetgelina," he whispered, and she saw a small hole in his chest, a tiny spot of blood on the pristine white of his shirt, standing out like a banner against a clear blue sky, as he slowly sank to his knees.

Her stomach hit the ground. "Oh no. No, David." She dropped to her knees, catching him as he sank down. She pulled him close. "Someone, get an ambulance. Man down!"

David grasped her shoulders. "I think I'm going to toss my cookies. I feel awful."

She ripped at his shirt as she shoved him down to the ground. "Not a bullet wound…"

"Stabbing."

"But small," she said and her face drained of color. "Poison," she whispered.

Frantically she looked around until she spotted the pen. "Bag that, Jacobs. We can use it to identify the poison."

David grabbed Angelina's hand. She realized she was gripping his shirt with both hands. "David, hang on."

"I love you. I will always love you," he whispered.

"Oh no…David," she moaned and in desperation she fell down on his chest, her face next to his. "You can't leave me. I can't lose you. I knew he'd go after you. Why did you let him stab you?"

"It was that or your president."

"So?" she said, her anger building. "He's been saved twice. You don't deserve this."

David stiffened and began to convulse.

Medics arrived.

Angelina lost it. "Someone do something! Help him!"

Jennings showed up and pulled her out of the way. "No! Let me go. I need to help him."

Jennings shook her. "You're not helping anyone. Stop it. Let them get him out of here. If you want to save him, tell me what you saw."

Angelina slapped at Jennings, but realized they were already loading David onto a stretcher. "Don't leave me, David," she cried out. "Don't leave me. I love you too."

They rushed out of the room with him.

"Come on," Jennings said and grabbed her arm. "The president is out of here and safe, thanks to you and your friend. Let's go make sure he's safe as well."

Angelina ran with Jennings, following the stretcher.

At the ambulance, Jennings stopped her. He

flagged down his car as the valet drove it up, and they piled into it. Her entire body trembled with a fear she couldn't describe. She'd never felt such dread. Her stomach churned and her vision blurred as she watched the ambulance pull away.

"Tell me what you saw at the house?" Jennings demanded, forcing Angelina's attention to him.

She jerked forward as the car jumped out into traffic. Angelina wracked her brain, holding onto the armrest as they swerved in and out of the midday traffic. "Plans. For the weapons. I realized it when I saw the president signing an autograph. You know there's always someone who wants his signature. There were pen parts. And chemicals. All kinds of chemicals."

Like clockwork, her mind went through all she'd seen. "Not in the cellar, but when he questioned me. In that room were chemicals—on a table."

One by one, she ticked them off as her mind went back over the room. She was suddenly very thankful for the questioning, as that had given her a chance to see so much. And with her mind, she rarely forgot a thing.

"That's it," Jennings suddenly said. "I think I know what we're dealing with."

"The tribunary," she said. "Because we know—"

Jennings shook his head. "I doubt they know you know about them or you would have been dead already. That name, however, is never again to be mentioned because we don't know who is involved or where their members are. I'm not surprised to find out Scorpion is a member, but we don't know everyone who is. And if you mention it around anyone in our business you just might disappear. So drop it."

"But—"

"I'm serious. This goes beyond us. You stick to this and if you want to see David alive again, you leave it to God to send someone who can break this group open."

Angelina blinked. "You're a Christian?"

He shrugged.

Before she could ask more about it, they pulled up at the hospital and Jennings jumped out.

She didn't follow him. She dismissed all he'd said deciding that would be for another day and another time. She got out of the vehicle and ran to the ambulance, however, David wasn't there. So she went into the hospital and waited, and while she was there, she prayed. For the first time in her life, she found comfort in prayer.

It seemed like hours before Jennings showed up, and, indeed, it was already dark out when she finally took notice. He had Walters and Stravinsky with him.

"The president is safe and word has been put out there was a bomb threat so they emptied the building. Of course, no one will really know about Frank's attempt on our friend's life."

Angelina nodded.

"Have you eaten?" Stravinsky asked and shoved coffee at her.

She shook her head. "I'm still waiting for word about David."

"We just got notified that he's out of danger and in a special wing here."

Relief flooded her, and she collapsed into a chair.

"Whoa, Harding," Walters said and reached out to steady her.

Her knees shook. "Thank you, thank you, thank you," she prayed and couldn't even express the relief she felt.

Then she popped back up. "I have to see him."

"He's in a special ICU area."

"I don't care, Jennings. I have to see him now."

Jennings scowled and said gruffly, "You can.

But I don't want you leaving until we've debriefed you."

"Where is he?" She shoved the coffee back at Stravinsky.

"Down the hall, take a right and tell them I sent you. They'll let you in. It's a secure wing for special patients we deem to need security while here."

She nodded and rushed from the waiting room down the hall.

She ignored those she passed, intent on finding David.

Within minutes, she was in the secure wing and at David's room, but once there, she found herself hesitating. She hadn't allowed herself to be vulnerable, not since her uncle, not since Scorpion.

But with David—

She had to make a decision.

She could turn now and leave, and she knew David wouldn't follow her once he was released. He'd understand she'd made her decision.

Or she could step through that door and her life would change forever.

She knew David loved her.

And she loved him.

But could she commit to that love and trust him?

"Angelina?"

She heard his voice and realized he must have seen her.

She pushed the door the rest of the way open. "How did you know it was me?" she asked, standing in the doorway.

"I could smell your perfume," he said weakly, a smile on his face.

She stared at him. "You look so good," she said, aching.

"You do too," he said and lifted an arm.

She hesitated a moment more and then stepped through the door, went straight to the bed and into his arms. "Oh, David, I love you."

She started crying.

"Well it's about time you realized that," David murmured into her hair.

She crawled onto the bed with him and hugged him. "I almost lost you."

"Never, my love. God brought us together for a reason, and He wasn't going to let me die before my time."

"I lost my brother, but I just couldn't lose you, too."

She was still crying when she heard, from the other side of the room. "Well, not exactly."

Her head popped up and only then did she realize her brother lay in a bed as well. She blinked twice, trying to make sure she wasn't imagining what she was seeing.

"I'm really here, sis."

She pulled out of David's arms and ran around the bed to where her brother lay. "How did you get here? Why? When?"

Marcus grunted as his sister hit him full-force in the chest. "Watch it, sis, I'm still pretty weak."

"I'm sorry," she whispered and kissed her brother on the cheek, hugging him tightly.

"And to answer your question, long before the president was shot, though I only really woke up about an hour ago." He yawned. "I'm on so many meds now that I can't really focus much."

"How—I don't understand."

"Some man named Hooter found me and then I was in this airplane and the next thing I remember was waking up here and seeing David in the same room."

"What a sight to wake up to," David murmured groggily.

Angelina kissed her brother again and brushed his hair back. Marcus blinked sleepily and said, "So, are you disappointed that I'm still alive and going to be able to give you away?"

"Never," she whispered, "if, that is, I can find someone who wants me."

Marcus chuckled even as he drifted off to sleep.

Angelina went back over to David and studied him carefully. "If I can find the *right* person who wants me, that is."

David blinked slowly and then shifted. "And what would be the qualifications?"

"Well,' she said. "He'd have to be a gentle giant who could handle any storm clouds that might come his way."

David nodded.

"He'd have to be willing to go back with me to America for a short time, as I think there's some unfinished business my boss might need help with."

David nodded again.

"And he'd have to work with me to help me heal and learn more about Someone I just met recently."

David grinned slowly and opened his arms. "And who would that be?"

"A carpenter, I'm told. Someone who worked with wood and was eventually nailed to that wood."

She climbed back up on the edge of the bed and David wrapped his arms around her, saying, "And *I'll* need someone who is going to be by me day by day, working with me as I walk the streets and listening to me as I stand in a pulpit. Someone who, for better or worse, is willing to spend the rest of my life with me. Know anyone who might qualify for that?"

"Hmm…" Angelina said, and wrapped her arms tightly about David. Tenderly, her eyes touched every part of his lovely face, and then softly, ever so gently, she whispered, "I do indeed," and leaned up to kiss him. Then lifting her lips, she met his gaze, her eyes filled with joy. "I do, indeed, my love."

Dear Reader,

Wow, do you have any idea the hundreds and hundreds of letters and e-mails I've received begging me to write Angelina's and Todd's stories? Guess what? I've wanted to write them, too—especially Angelina's. She tried to take over in *Shelter from the Storm,* so I had to send her to Australia. And here is her story.

She is such a strong woman that she wore me out trying to write about her. I fell absolutely in love with this stalwart yet vulnerable woman. We all have pasts, no matter how innocent, because at one time we were all without the knowledge of God's love and forgiveness. And in Angelina, we see how sometimes we just can't learn to let go of the past, forget about it and strive onward, toward the goal that God has set for us—and that is Jesus Christ. If you hurt or have pain, please let it go and let God show you His love. Know that God will use those things to shape us and form us so that we can do His work as he did with Angelina. He loves you, dear one, and He won't ever leave you.

I love to hear from readers, and I now live in Oklahoma. If you write to me, please be sure to make note of my new address: P.O. Box 106, Faxon, OK 73540, though my e-mail address remains the same: Cheryl@cherylwolverton.com.

In Christ's love,

Cheryl Wolverton

Love Inspired SUSPENSE
RIVETING INSPIRATIONAL ROMANCE

Coming in November...

Her Brother's Keeper

by Valerie Hansen

An ordained minister turned undercover investigator is on a mission to uncover the truth about a young woman's past. But can he do that without hurting the woman he's come to love?

Available at your favorite retail outlet.
Only from Steeple Hill Books!

Steeple Hill®

www.SteepleHill.com

LISHBK

Take 2 inspirational love stories FREE!

PLUS get a FREE surprise gift!

Mail to Steeple Hill Reader Service™

In U.S.
3010 Walden Ave.
P.O. Box 1867
Buffalo, NY 14240-1867

In Canada
P.O. Box 609
Fort Erie, Ontario
L2A 5X3

YES! Please send me 2 free Love Inspired® novels and my free surprise gift. After receiving them, if I don't wish to receive anymore, I can return the shipping statement marked cancel. If I don't cancel, I will receive 4 brand-new novels every month, before they're available in stores! Bill me at the low price of $4.24 each in the U.S. and $4.74 each in Canada, plus 25¢ shipping and handling and applicable sales tax, if any*. That's the complete price and a savings of over 10% off the cover prices—quite a bargain! I understand that accepting the books and gift places me under no obligation ever to buy any books. I can always return a shipment and cancel at any time. Even if I never buy another book from Steeple Hill, the 2 free books and the surprise gift are mine to keep forever.

113 IDN DZ9M
313 IDN DZ9N

Name	(PLEASE PRINT)	
Address	Apt. No.	
City	State/Prov.	Zip/Postal Code

Not valid to current Love Inspired® subscribers.

Want to try two free books from another series?
Call 1-800-873-8635 or visit www.morefreebooks.com.

* Terms and prices are subject to change without notice. Sales tax applicable in New York. Canadian residents will be charged applicable provincial taxes and GST. All orders subject to approval. Offer limited to one per household.

® are registered trademarks owned and used by the trademark owner and or its licensee.

INTLI04R   ©2004 Steeple Hill

Love Inspired™

IN THE SPIRIT OF... CHRISTMAS

BY

LINDA GOODNIGHT

Jesse Slater was raising his traumatized little girl, trying to reclaim his family's farm...and dealing with bitter memories of past holiday seasons. He didn't count on falling for his temporary boss Lindsey Mitchell. Lindsey sensed there were reasons behind Jesse's lack of faith, and wondered if she was meant to teach him and his daughter the true meaning of Christmas....

Don't miss IN THE SPIRIT OF...CHRISTMAS
On sale November 2005

Available at your favorite retail outlet.

Love Inspired®
SUSPENSE

TITLES AVAILABLE NEXT MONTH

Don't miss these two stories in November

SHADOW BONES by Colleen Rhoads
Great Lakes Legends

Skye Blackbird was convinced she'd find diamonds in her
family's mine. Paleontologist Jake Baxter felt the same
about fossils. When the site was sabotaged, Jake didn't
know who to blame. Someone didn't want the earth
disturbed, but it also seemed that someone might
not want him or Skye alive...

HER BROTHER'S KEEPER by Valerie Hansen

Becky Tate finds the new preacher charming. But though
he's ordained, Logan Malloy has never preached before!
He's undercover, investigating whether Becky was kidnapped
as an infant. He has to find the truth without ruining the
only family Becky knows—and hurting the woman he's
come to love....

LISCNM1005